A BABY FOR
DRY CREEK

JANET TRONSTAD

Published by Steeple Hill Books™

STEEPLE HILL BOOKS

Steeple
Hill®

ISBN 0-373-87250-X

A BABY FOR DRY CREEK

Copyright © 2004 by Janet Tronstad

Visit us at www.steeplehill.com

Printed in U.S.A.

"For I was hungry and you gave me food;
I was thirsty and you gave me drink;
I was a stranger and you took me in."
—*Matthew* 25:35

This book is dedicated with many fond memories to my forty cousins, both the Norris side of the family and the Tronstad side of the family. Thanks for the good times!

Prologue

Chrissy Hamilton figured her life couldn't get much worse. On the morning of what was supposed to be her wedding day, she had found another woman in her fiancé's bed. And that wasn't even the worst part. After she'd stomped out of Jared's bedroom and driven almost all the way to Dry Creek, Montana, in her cousin's truck, she'd met a man who made her knees melt so fast she wouldn't have cared if an entire cheerleading squad had been camped out in Jared's bed.

Of course, nothing could come of her attraction. She was two and a half months pregnant and just about as confused and miserable as an eighteen-year-old in trouble could be.

Besides, if Chrissy couldn't trust the man she'd

loved since she was fifteen, she certainly wasn't going to risk trusting some Montana rancher she'd just met.

It was too bad about the rancher, though. With his black hair and sky blue eyes, Reno Redfern was the sexiest man she'd ever seen. Which was one more reason to leave Dry Creek.

Seven and a half months later

Dry Creek did not have a postmaster. It didn't even have a post office. Everyone knew that. Still, the letter addressed to the postmaster sat there on top of all the other letters the mail carrier had left on the counter of the hardware store this cold spring morning. The mail carrier hadn't even looked at the letter before crawling back into the postal truck and heading down Interstate 94 to the next small Montana town on his busy route.

The hardware store sold everything a rancher needed, from weed killer to waterproof gloves, and most of it was sitting on long wooden shelves that lined the walls. A stack of ceramic mugs stood on a cart beside the stockroom door and the smell of brewing coffee welcomed customers every day of the week except Sunday, when the store was closed.

Of course, not everyone was a customer. The hardware store served as an informal community center, and some retired ranchers, like Jacob, spent most of their waking hours there arguing about cattle prices and waiting for the mail.

"Who'd be writing to our postmaster?" Jacob asked as he lifted the first envelope and read the address. He had been a rancher for sixty of his seventy-seven years, and his gnarled fingers showed it as he held up the letter.

"We don't have a postmaster." Mrs. Hargrove also waited for the mail. She didn't sit, like the men, preferring to stand on the rubber mat by the counter so her muddy boots didn't dirty the wood floor as the men's boots were doing. She would rather distribute the mail herself, since she could do it more efficiently than Jacob, but she was a fair-minded woman and Jacob had gotten to the mail counter first.

In addition to Mrs. Hargrove, a half dozen ranchers were waiting for their mail, and the door was opening to let more into the store. Each time the door swung back or forth, a gust of wind came inside. As usual, spring had started out cold, but everyone had expected it to warm up by now. Most of the ranchers said they could still smell winter in the air and they didn't like it. They should be planting their fields, and it was too muddy to even plow.

"We might not have a postmaster, but we got us a letter," Jacob said as he put the envelope up to the light and tried to see through it before lowering his eyes and looking around at the others. "From a law firm. In California."

"What would a law firm want with our postmaster? We haven't broken any laws." Another retired rancher, Elmer, spoke up from where he sat by the black woodstove that stood in the middle of the hardware store. The morning was chilly enough that a small fire was burning inside the stove.

As he was speaking, Elmer stood up and frowned.

The inside of the hardware store got quiet as Elmer slowly walked toward the counter. The people of Dry Creek had a large respect for the law and an equally large distrust of California lawyers. They also knew that Elmer had an instinct for trouble, and if he was worried enough to leave his chair, they were worried, too.

"I keep telling folks we need to get a more regular way of sorting the mail," said a middle-aged rancher, Lester, as he looked up from the bolts he was sorting along the far wall. He scowled as he took up the old argument. "You're not supposed to see other folks' mail—it's not legal. The FBI can get involved."

"The FBI has better things to worry about than who sees your seed catalogs," Elmer said as he finished walking over to Jacob and looked down at the letter the other man still held. "Besides, no one in California would care how we sort through our mail. Would they?"

"Well, open it up and read it to us," Mrs. Hargrove finally said. She had a raisin bread pudding baking in her oven and she didn't want the crust to get too brown. "We haven't got all morning."

Jacob took out his pocketknife and used it as a letter opener. Then he cleared his throat and carefully read the entire letter aloud word by word. Jacob had always been proud of his speaking abilities, and he hadn't had many chances in his life for public performances. If there hadn't been so many people gathered in the hardware store, he probably would have listened to what he was saying instead of just focusing on getting all the words spoken correctly and loudly the way Mrs. Baker, his first-grade teacher, would have expected.

> Joseph K. Price, Attorney-at-Law
> 918 Green Street, Suite 200
> Pasadena, California 91104

Dear Dry Creek Postmaster,
I'm writing to request your help in locating a man who lives in your community. Unfortunately, I do not know the man's full name, so I cannot write to him directly. The nature of my business is this man's relationship with a young woman, Chrissy Hamilton, and her new baby. It is the paternity of the infant that I wish to establish.

Miss Hamilton was in your community last fall. I am hopeful you will know the young man who spent the night with Miss Hamilton in her cousin's truck. The man's first name is Reno. If you can supply me with the man's full name, I assure you that my client, Mrs. Bard, will be happy to reward you (you have no doubt heard of the family—they own the national chain of dry cleaners by the same name). I realize this is an unusual request, and I want to assure you that no one is asking the man to assume financial responsibility for the baby. Quite the opposite, in fact. Mrs. Bard is anxious to adopt the baby should it be proven to her satisfaction that her son, Jared, is the baby's father. I apologize for the unorthodox nature of this request. It would not be necessary if Miss Hamilton were more cooperative. But she is young (eighteen, I believe) and does not yet see the full advantage to herself in this arrangement. I look forward to hearing from you soon.

> Yours truly,
> Joseph K. Price, Esq.

The whole store listened and then stood still in stunned silence for a moment.

Finally Elmer spoke. "Our Reno?"

"Nothing says Reno's the baby's father," Mrs. Hargrove cautioned, and then her voice softened. "Imagine, a baby."

"Where is Reno, anyway?" Elmer looked around. "He's usually here to get his mail by now."

Chapter One

Reno Redfern stopped his pickup in front of the hardware store in Dry Creek. He was late and splattered with thick gray mud. Hopefully someone would have sorted the mail by now, and he could quietly pick up his few bills and get back to the ranch and shower. If he had been paying more attention to the road, he wouldn't have slipped into the ditch and ended up with the wheels of his pickup stuck in the mud.

Reno shook his head. He'd made it a point to thank God repeatedly for the rain—what rancher wouldn't?—but he was working on being honest in his dealings with God, and so far he hadn't been able to say anything polite about the mud. The mud just lay everywhere, making the ground look forlorn and generally being a nuisance.

Reno had liked the first part of spring well enough. The cold of winter had eased up a little and he could walk from the house to the barn without pulling his cap down over his ears. But later, for some reason, everything had turned to mud. The mountains were no longer covered in snow, but the grass hadn't taken hold yet either. Gray clouds hung in most of the skies, and the air was wet even when it wasn't raining. The worst part was the deep clay that trapped everyone's wheels.

Reno frowned as he opened the door to his pickup. The one good thing he could say for the mud was that it matched his mood these days. If it had been a normal Montana spring with endless blue sky and those tiny purple wildflowers blooming beside the gravel roads, he wouldn't have been able to take all the love and sunshine flowing around the Redfern Ranch now that his sister, Nicki, had settled into married life.

At first Reno had wondered in alarm if he were jealous of Nicki's wedded bliss. But that wasn't it. He just missed the way things used to be.

There was such a thing as too much happiness, Reno finally decided, and his sister proved it. Nicki was so sweet these days it made his teeth ache. If she weren't so sweet, he probably wouldn't miss the old Nicki so much.

But as much as he tried to bring Nicki back to her senses, he couldn't. He couldn't even get her going on a good argument about cattle prices and fertilizer, and those used to be her favorite topics for heated discussion. But now all she wanted to talk about was curtain fabric and love. She had a perfectly good rancher's brain that was turning to sentimental mush, and he was powerless to stop it.

And she wasn't content to limit her new sentimental thoughts of love to herself and her new husband. Oh, no—she had started to speak of marriage with a missionary zeal that made Reno nervous. He had seen the speculation in her eyes several days before she came right out and asked him if he'd like her to set him up.

Set him up! Reno still couldn't believe it. He and Nicki had had a pact. Neither one of them was going to get married, at least not for love. Of course, they'd made that vow when they were ten and twelve, a good four years after their mother had left their father and they'd heard every day since about the damage love could do from their father's own bitter lips.

Besides, even if Reno decided to take leave of his senses and look for a wife, he didn't need his sister doing the looking for him. There were plenty of women who wanted to date him. Granted, he wasn't exactly in touch with any of them at the moment, but that was only because he was busy feeding the new calves and, well—things.

"I'm getting around to it." Reno had set his glass of water down on the kitchen counter when Nicki asked her question. "You don't need to worry about me. I'm doing fine."

''Really, you've met someone you want to date?''

Reno scowled. She didn't need to sound so surprised. ''Well, no, but I will—''

''When you have time,'' Nicki finished for him, and shook her head. ''I know as well as you do that there's never any extra time when you're ranching— you have to make time for what's important.''

''Getting the alfalfa planted is important.''

''With mud like this, you can't even plow. That's why Garrett and I decided to go to Denver. There's nothing to do right now.''

''I can change the plugs on the tractor.''

''Or you could do something fun for a change, like maybe go down to Los Angeles and pay a visit to Chrissy Hamilton.''

Reno was struck dumb. Chrissy was the cousin of Nicki's new husband, Garrett Hamilton. ''Why would I do that?''

''Because you've been, well, morose since Chrissy visited here last fall. That's not like you.''

Morose? Ever since Nicki had married her trucker husband, she'd started learning a new word every day. Reno didn't like to discourage anyone who wanted to learn. Still… ''That's not because of Chrissy.''

Well, Reno admitted to himself, it might be a little bit because of Chrissy, but it wasn't in the way his sister thought.

Chrissy had come to Dry Creek last fall looking for Reno and Nicki's mother. Before Chrissy moved back to Los Angeles, she had been a waitress in the Las

Vegas casino where their mother worked. The two
had become friends, and Reno could understand why.

If Chrissy was upsetting to him, it was only because she reminded him of his mother. Both women
had that high-wattage, bright-color sway that went
with a place like Las Vegas. They wore fancy sequin
dresses with the same ease that women in Dry Creek
wore their aprons.

It was clear that neither his mother nor Chrissy be-
longed in Dry Creek, and that's why Chrissy had
bothered him. Really the only reason she still bothered him, he told himself.

Nicki looked at him as if she didn't believe him.
"You're not still afraid to get married, are you?"

"Huh?"

Nicki had the grace to blush. "I know we both said
we would never get married, but we were kids. What
did we know?"

"We knew what Dad told us."

"Ah, well, he only saw one side of being married.
If he'd known there were people out there like Garrett, who can really love someone, he wouldn't have
wanted us to stay single all our lives."

Reno decided he shouldn't argue with his sister on
this one. "I suppose he might have been okay with
you marrying."

Nicki looked relieved. "And you, too."

Reno doubted all of it. He had known his father.
But he held his tongue.

"Anyway, here's Chrissy's address and phone

number,'' Nicki said as she pulled a piece of paper out of her jeans pocket and set it on the kitchen counter. ''You could at least call and talk to her—or write her a letter or something.''

With that, Nicki turned and walked away.

She might as well have left a stick of live dynamite on the kitchen counter.

Reno just stared at the paper.

He didn't tell his sister that he didn't need to call Chrissy or write her a letter to find out if the two of them were destined for some kind of wedded bliss. For even a little bit of bliss to happen, the woman would have to like him, and it appeared the very thought of dating him made Chrissy Hamilton want to cry.

Even someone as lovestruck as his sister would have to agree that was not a good sign. Fortunately, no one knew about him and Chrissy.

When Chrissy had been at the ranch last fall, he'd decided to invite her to eat dinner at the café in Dry Creek with him. He hadn't thought it was any big deal. He'd spent the afternoon convincing himself that just because her green-gray eyes made him want to take up painting storm clouds, that was no reason to think he was interested in anything but getting to know someone who could tell him more about his mother.

He'd even stopped himself from wondering about Chrissy's lips once he decided they looked as soft as they did because of some sort of Las Vegas beauty trick.

No, he'd put all that aside. Dinner was just a logical thing. Hamburgers and fries for two hungry people at the café in Dry Creek. Maybe spaghetti and garlic bread, if they had it. He'd started out by saying there was no reason to go to any trouble and change clothes and they both had to eat, so would she like to come with him to eat at the—

That's as far as he'd got before she'd given him a stricken look and started to cry. He hadn't known what to do but take her in his arms and let her sob against his last clean shirt. After the first burst of tears had ended, she'd pulled back and looked embarrassed. Her cheeks had been pink, and her eyes had dared him to ask about her tears.

Before he could say anything, she'd thanked him for the invitation in a businesslike voice and added she was sorry she couldn't date him. She was also sorry about the shirt, she said, and added that a little bleach should take the mascara out.

By then he couldn't say he hadn't been asking her out on a date, so he'd just thanked her for the laundry tip. He hadn't added that he was surprised. He'd never figured someone like Chrissy would know anything about laundry.

Fortunately, no one knew about any of this, and Reno wasn't about to tell anyone. He picked up the slip of paper from the kitchen counter, intending to crumple it up and throw it away. He should be glad Chrissy wasn't interested in him.

Reno was cautious when it came to women. Even if he hadn't had his father to remind him of how fickle women could be, his mother had taught him that some women just weren't meant to live on a ranch.

Life on the Redfern Ranch could never compete with the excitement of a big city. Ranch life was plain, good living, and that was all Reno wanted, but he knew there was no theater, no fine dining, no museums, no upscale shopping.

A Vegas cocktail waitress like Chrissy would never stay in a place like Dry Creek any more than his mother had. Oh, Chrissy might think it was quaint and amusing enough for a week or so, but in the long term she'd leave. Dry Creek would never be enough for her.

Yes, throwing away that piece of paper his sister had left on the counter was the only sensible thing to do. Reno said those words to himself, but for some strange reason he didn't listen. Instead, he folded the piece of paper into a small square and put it in his shirt pocket.

He told himself he'd throw it away tomorrow. When tomorrow came, he told himself it wouldn't hurt to wait until the next day.

That was two weeks ago Monday, and he no longer even bothered to lie to himself. Every day when he changed his shirt, he moved that piece of paper to the new pocket.

Reno shook his head. This past Saturday he'd actually looked at a map to see which freeways he'd need to take if he drove down to Los Angeles. He'd gone so far as to remind himself he'd never seen the Pacific Ocean and had a good reason to drive down to Los Angeles, quite apart from seeing Chrissy. A man ought to see the ocean some time in his life.

Reno scraped his feet on the porch of the hardware store. At least no one in Dry Creek knew about that slip of paper in his pocket or the foolish thoughts going around in his head. He wouldn't have had any peace if they did. Sometimes it felt as if he had a dozen grandparents, each one of them anxious for him to date someone so they could plan a wedding and then begin the more serious business of knitting baby booties.

Reno didn't know why the seniors in Dry Creek were so set on babies. But all he heard these days were wistful remarks that, given all the marriages in Dry Creek lately, it sure was a shame there weren't any babies.

No, he didn't want the people of Dry Creek to know he was even thinking of visiting Chrissy. They'd start putting their hopes on him, and he'd only let them down.

Chapter Two

Reno opened the door. The hardware store was silent, and for a brief second the light was such that Reno thought no one was inside. Then he saw all his neighbors, and they saw him. It was a toss-up as to who was more startled.

"It's that clay mud," Reno finally said as he stepped inside. They were looking at him as if he were covered with tar or something toxic. "I guess I look a little odd."

"You look just fine," Mrs. Hargrove declared stoutly as she smoothed down the skirt of her checked gingham dress. Mrs. Hargrove had to be eighty years old, and she'd worn the same set of gingham dresses since the late 1950s. She had one in every color of the rainbow. A good dress, she told folks, never wore out as long as you took care of it. Over the dress she wore a black wool sweater that had been stretched out by too many washes. She had rubber boots on her feet and a paperback mystery stuffed into the pocket of her sweater.

Reno stopped and stood still. If Mrs. Hargrove had to defend him that strongly, he must look worse than he thought. She'd been his Sunday-school teacher years ago, and she was loyal to her students. He'd been in the first grade when he'd realized that she fussed with her hair or her dress on the few occasions she was nervous. She'd done it when Randy McCall asked where Eve got her babies from, and she was doing it now.

Mrs. Hargrove reached up and patted her gray hair to make sure her bun was secure. She could have saved herself the effort. Mrs. Hargrove's hair wouldn't dare misbehave, any more than the first-grade boys would have years ago.

"If someone will just hand me my mail, I'll step back to the porch," Reno offered as he looked down. He must have left giant tracks on the clean floor or something, but the floor was already muddy, and not with his footprints. "I'll have to remember this one for April Fools' Day. I don't think Lester got this much of a reaction when he dressed up like Elvis and went to the café for breakfast. Who would have thought he was that much of a clown?"

Lester stood up from where he was kneeling beside the bottom bin of the nail rack. He was a short, wiry man who seldom spoke, and he cleared his throat before he started to talk. "I may be a clown sometimes, but at least I would financially support a baby if I had fathered one."

"Huh?" Reno wondered if he had missed something. Lester was Reno's closest neighbor, and he looked as if he'd screwed up all his courage to speak. "Since when do you have a baby?"

"Sometimes a man can have a baby and not even know it."

At least six people in the room sucked in their breath.

"Hush, now," Mrs. Hargrove finally managed to say. "It's none of our business. Just because we're all used to seeing everyone's mail as it comes in, it's no reason to meddle."

Reno wondered what she was talking about. Everyone in Dry Creek meddled. It was one of their most endearing traits. It meant they cared.

"That letter was addressed to us," Jacob said indignantly. "We weren't reading anything but what was meant for us. We're the ones who take turns passing out the mail in Dry Creek. We're the postmaster."

"Still," Elmer muttered as he walked back to his chair by the stove, "it's not our business. Of course, in my day a young man was raised to do the honorable thing and marry a woman he got with child."

"Lester got someone pregnant?" Reno finally asked. The last he knew, Lester had been courting

Nicki. That was before she married Garrett, of course, but still Reno didn't like to think of Lester playing his sister false. "I thought you were planning on marrying Nicki."

If Reno's voice rose a little, he figured no one could blame him. A man was supposed to defend his sister's honor, even if she was off being a trucker along with her new husband.

Lester took a step forward. "Not me, you fool. You're the one with the baby."

Lester could as well have said that Reno had a castle in Spain or a boot growing out of his head. *"What?"*

"Now, remember the letter didn't say that Reno was the one," Mrs. Hargrove cautioned. "For all we know, he didn't even have those kinds of thoughts about Chrissy Hamilton. The Reno I know is a good boy."

Reno choked. He wished he had a little more mud covering his face so no one could see his guilty flush. How did you tell your old Sunday-school teacher that you'd stopped being a boy a dozen years ago? He sure didn't want to start telling Mrs. Hargrove about the jumble of thoughts he had about Chrissy Hamilton.

Even though he knew Chrissy wasn't the one for him, he still found her attractive. Well, maybe more than attractive, if he was strictly honest about it. Something about Chrissy reminded him of the time as a boy he had been fascinated by a picture of cobras in some catalog that had come to the ranch.

Not that Reno was worried. He had been smart enough not to order a cobra from that catalog when he was nine years old and he was smart enough now to avoid Chrissy. Just because he was drawn to both of them in some mysterious, crazy way didn't mean he had to do anything about it.

Besides, Mrs. Hargrove was right about one thing. It wasn't anyone else's business anyway.

"Chrissy is a fine-looking girl," Elmer volunteered as he sat down in his chair by the stove. His voice was thoughtful. "Reno would have to be blind not to see that."

"Well, that's true," Mrs. Hargrove conceded before she turned back to Reno. "But that doesn't mean he's the father of her baby."

"Chrissy has a baby?" Reno felt the streak of mud start to dry and crack on his face. His voice had grown hoarse and he had to clear his throat. He felt a strange disappointment. "I suppose she's married to that Jared fellow by now, then."

Jacob frowned as he looked down at the letter in his hand. "Doesn't sound like she's married to anyone."

Reno had known Jacob all his life. The man had taught him how to rope a calf. But Reno didn't believe him on this one. Chrissy might have been mad at her boyfriend when she was in Dry Creek, but Jared had significant money, and a woman like Chrissy would weigh that in the scales before she called it off. Reno figured there was some misunderstanding. He held his hand out for the letter. "Let me see."

Jacob handed him the letter.

There was silence for a minute before Mrs. Hargrove said, "You know, maybe one of us should write to Chrissy and invite her to come to Dry Creek with her baby."

Reno snorted. He didn't want to hurt Mrs. Hargrove's feelings, but Chrissy would probably rather move to the moon than to Dry Creek. She likely thought it was the backside of nowhere, and she was right. Just because the people of Dry Creek liked the middle of nowhere didn't mean Chrissy would. "We don't have any shows or nightclubs or anything. Shoot, we don't even have a proper post office."

Reno returned to reading the letter.

"We have the café," Jacob answered. "And the Christmas pageant every year."

"Pastor Matthew's sermons have been downright entertaining lately with some of his stories about the twins," Mrs. Hargrove added. "I think he's almost as funny as that guy on the television everyone talks about. Any new mother would enjoy that."

"She could play with those calves of yours, too," Jacob added. "They're pretty cute—especially the ones you're feeding with that fancy bucket of yours."

Reno looked up from the letter. He had finished it.

"Well, she should be happy. Sounds like she's going to get a handsome payment."

"Reno Redfern!" Mrs. Hargrove said. "I can't believe you think that sweet girl would give her baby up to that lawyer!"

"Well, she wouldn't be giving it to the lawyer. The baby would go to Mrs. Bard. How bad can living with your grandmother be?"

Reno couldn't help but wish he'd had a grandmother who would have taken care of him when his mother left. "She probably bakes cookies and everything. The baby will be fine."

Mrs. Hargrove drew herself up indignantly. "Don't you know anything about a mother's love?" Then she gasped and put her hand over her mouth. "I'm sorry. I wasn't thinking."

Reno forced himself to smile. "That's okay."

It wasn't Mrs. Hargrove's fault his mother had left him and Nicki when she left their father. It wasn't anyone's fault. Not all women were good mothers.

"I should have insisted that father of yours bring you to town more often when your mother left," Mrs. Hargrove muttered. "Just because the two of you looked fine, I shouldn't have assumed your poor little hearts weren't broken."

"Nothing was broken," Reno said. "Lots of people have it worse in life."

Reno had made his peace with the fact that his

mother had left when he was six. He'd had his father and he'd had Nicki. He'd done just fine.

"But still—"

"I'm sure Chrissy and her baby will be fine." Reno wasn't sure which topic he wanted to discuss less, his mother or Chrissy.

Mrs. Hargrove nodded. "Still, if they were to come here—"

"I'm sure she doesn't want to move here," Reno repeated.

"Well, still, there's the baby to think about. It's our Christian duty to at least invite Chrissy. Someone needs to write her a letter and ask. It's the hospitable thing to do for someone in trouble and—and—I'm beginning to think that's what God would want. He always said we should offer hospitality to the stranger who's in trouble."

Reno looked at his former Sunday-school teacher. She was eyeing him the way she had in the first grade when she wanted volunteers to answer a question. She wasn't playing fair by bringing God into this, and she probably knew it.

"I think God was talking about feeding strangers when they show up in town and are hungry. So far every person who drives through Dry Creek seems to be pretty well fed. But if they're not, I'll leave word with Linda and Jazz at the café to give them something to eat and add it to my bill."

Mrs. Hargrove frowned. "Hospitality is about more

than food—God also told us to take in people who are in trouble.''

''Well, God usually brings them to your doorstep. Chrissy is thousands of miles away.''

''I didn't think of that,'' Mrs. Hargrove said. ''We can't just write a letter. How will she get here?''

''She's not coming.'' Reno ground his teeth and searched for a change of subject. ''Lots of mud outside, isn't there?''

No one answered him.

''You know, Reno has a point, though,'' Jacob agreed. ''Usually God would do something to give a person a clue. Even Reno can't just go driving down there to bring her and the baby back here. He doesn't have the poor girl's address.''

Reno reached up to make sure the pocket on his shirt wasn't on fire. Keeping quiet wasn't exactly a lie, but he didn't want to deceive anyone. ''Well, even supposing I did have an address for her, people in Los Angeles move around all the time. How long would an address be good, anyway?''

Jacob frowned as he pointed to the letter Reno still held. ''Come to think of it, I bet that attorney would have her current address. Sounds like he's keeping a close eye on her.''

Mrs. Hargrove nodded. ''It's settled, then. Someone will have to go see if Chrissy wants to come here.''

"I'll go," Lester volunteered from where he stood counting nails to put into a brown paper bag.

Reno looked at Lester suspiciously. The man had an eagerness about him that Reno didn't trust. "It's a long way down to Los Angeles."

Lester grinned. "Yeah, but it's a long way back, too. If she says she'll come back here, I figure it'll give me time to court her."

"What? She's half your age," Reno said. "You can't date her."

"She's single." Lester looked surprised. "I'm single. What's your problem? She's not that much younger than your sister, and you didn't object to me dating Nicki. Besides, some women like older men."

"No, Reno's right," Mrs. Hargrove said. "We can't be sending some man down there who's going to make her nervous. We need to send someone safe. Like Reno. He wouldn't ask her out. Why, he's almost family, now that I think of it."

"Almost family—" Reno choked.

"She's Garrett's cousin," Mrs. Hargrove explained patiently. "Garrett is married to your sister. That means Chrissy is almost your cousin."

Almost cousins. Reno groaned. It wasn't fair. Family was the cornerstone of the Redfern Ranch and it had been for generations. Mrs. Hargrove knew he'd never refuse to help someone who could claim to be family. If he did, he'd be breaking one of those family rules that the Redferns had held on to since the turn of the past century.

Reno gritted his teeth. Usually he was proud and grateful to be part of a family that had lived on the same land for so long. But sometimes, like today, the rules of the family were not ones he wanted to keep.

"And she's got that poor little boy with only half of his rightful parents," Mrs. Hargrove continued, as though she were just chatting.

This time Reno did groan aloud. He had a weakness for babies who didn't have a full set of parents. This wasn't a family rule; it was all his own.

"All right, I'll go," Reno said before his good sense kicked in.

"What about those calves of yours?" Lester asked. "With your sister and that new husband of hers gone, there won't be anyone there to feed them."

"Oh." Reno had forgotten about the calves. Usually when a set of twin calves was born, one of the two was a runt that was visibly smaller and weaker than the other calf. The mother would often ignore the runt and feed only the stronger calf. The Redfern Ranch had a bumper crop of twins this year, and it took Reno four or five hours a day just to keep the runts fed.

Some ranchers figured the runts were too much trouble to keep alive and left them to live or die as nature saw fit. But Reno didn't agree with nature on this one. He always brought the runts into the barn and fed them a special formula from a bucket he'd made that had an agricultural nipple so the calves could nurse easily.

Keeping those calves healthy was one of the most satisfying things he did as a rancher, and he'd long ago realized that he identified with the poor motherless things. He couldn't leave them. They'd die without regular feeding.

"I can see to them," Mrs. Hargrove said. "Do me good to get out on a farm again."

"There's no need. I can feed them," Lester said reluctantly. "If I'm not the one that goes to get Chrissy, I can do that much. That's what neighbors are for—especially when it's too wet to plow. Besides, it'll give Reno a chance to tell Chrissy what a good neighbor I've been."

Reno forced his lips into a smile. "You're the best."

"Good." Mrs. Hargrove nodded as if it was settled. "Then Reno can bring Chrissy back."

"She might not want to come." Reno felt he should remind everyone of that fact. He certainly didn't intend to give Chrissy a sales pitch. He would make the offer to satisfy Mrs. Hargrove, but he didn't expect Chrissy to actually agree to it. "Los Angeles is her home."

"Oh, you'll convince her." Mrs. Hargrove smiled. "You could always get the other kids to do whatever you wanted."

"That was in the first grade."

Mrs. Hargrove nodded. "A boy never loses that kind of charm."

Reno grunted. He felt about as charming as the mud on his feet.

Mrs. Hargrove's smile wavered and she looked a little uncertain. "Well, at least you will be sincere. And tell her we have free sundaes at the café on Friday nights."

Reno doubted there was a woman anywhere who would move across three states just to get a free sundae. He turned to leave the store. He'd go back to the ranch and show Lester where the milk buckets were. "I'll be on my way in a couple of hours."

"Good." Mrs. Hargrove nodded and then cleared her throat. Her face went pink and she patted at her hair again. "You know, Reno, it's none of my business if you and Chrissy—you know—if you're the baby's father. I just want you to know that even if you and Chrissy got off on the wrong foot, God can still make a good life for the two of you if you let Him."

Reno pushed his cap down on his head. He didn't need to look around to know that every man in the hardware store was staring at the floor. They were all used to talking about calves being born and cows artificially inseminated. They weren't a delicate group. But none of them was comfortable talking about any of those activities with Mrs. Hargrove. He decided to spare everyone further speculation about his love life. "I'll call when I get down to Los Angeles. My pickup should make it in three days."

"Your pickup?" Mrs. Hargrove frowned. "You can't take your pickup. You need a back seat with seat belts for the baby's car seat. You'll have to borrow my car."

Mrs. Hargrove drove a 1971 Dodge compact the color of old mustard. It smelled of foot powder and wouldn't go faster than fifty miles an hour. The junk dealer in Miles City had given up offering Mrs. Hargrove cash for the car and grumbled he'd have to charge her a tow fee when she finally came to her senses and gave up on the old thing. Still, the car never refused to start, not even in thirty-below weather, and that was more than some of the newer cars did.

"I could rent a car," Reno said as his mind began to calculate the cost. Three days down and three days back. It was the price of the feed supplements he was giving those runt calves. Some years that would be fine. But this year money was tight.

"Don't be foolish. My car's sound as a tank. It'll get you there and back."

Reno frowned. If he had any lingering hopes that Chrissy would surprise him and want to move back to Dry Creek, Mrs. Hargrove's car would remind him how unlikely those hopes were. A stylish woman like Chrissy wouldn't go to her own funeral in Mrs. Hargrove's car. She certainly wouldn't pack up her belongings and ride across three states in it. "I'll take it. Thanks."

"Tell Chrissy she's in my prayers," Mrs. Hargrove said.

Reno nodded as he walked to the door. "I'll do that—if I get a chance."

He doubted he would be given a chance. Chrissy had not seemed drawn to the church when she was here last. He was pretty sure prayers would fall into the same category as mustard-colored cars when it came to women like Chrissy.

"I know she's never gone to church much," Mrs. Hargrove continued. "But now that she's a mother she might want to—be sure and tell her there's a good Sunday school program for the little one."

Reno had a sudden vision of Chrissy sitting beside him in a Dry Creek church pew and it made his mouth dry up with the shock of it. He shook his head to clear his mind. He didn't need something like that vision rattling around in his head.

The church in Dry Creek was a place of peace for him. After his mother visited the town last fall and Reno had started the process of forgiving her, he had been drawn to the church he'd last attended as a child.

Reno had never really stopped believing in God during those years when he didn't go to church. He'd just stayed home to keep his father from drinking. For some reason, his father had insisted Nicki attend church, but he'd given Reno a choice. When he'd realized his father was drinking when he was alone at the ranch, Reno had found reasons to stay home on Sunday.

Until now he hadn't thought about what it would feel like to sit in church with a wife beside him. Reno had a sudden empathy for the loneliness his father must have faced on those Sundays long ago after his wife left.

Reno cleared his throat. He was as bad as Mrs. Hargrove. He needed to keep reality in mind. ''She might decide not to come.''

''Use your charm.''

Reno grunted as he opened the door and stepped back out into the cold air. Fortunately he didn't need to worry about charm when it came to Chrissy. He wasn't likely to be given the chance to talk to her long enough to be charming. All he hoped was that he had enough time to give the invitation from Mrs. Hargrove so that he could honestly tell everyone he'd asked the question. That's all Mrs. Hargrove and God could expect.

Chapter Three

Chrissy looked out the big windows of Pete's Diner to the busy street outside. Something was making her edgy today, and not even the steady pace of orders from Pete's regulars could keep her mind focused. It must be because she'd seen that funny cap this morning. The man wearing the cap had told her he was from North Dakota. She smiled, because it was the same kind of cap that Reno wore in Dry Creek, Montana.

Whatever possessed her to remember that cap she didn't know. She also didn't know why the cap was so appealing. She'd always thought a Stetson on the head of a cowboy was the only kind of hat that would make a woman's heart race; but that farmer's cap that Reno had worn made her question all she knew about men's headwear.

If someone had told her she'd fall for a man in a cap, she would have said they were crazy. Especially a forest-green cap that advertised a yellow tractor, of all things!

But the cap sat on Reno's head, and that made all the difference. Reno had the chiseled bone structure of a Greek statue and the smooth grace of a man who was used to working outdoors. He wasn't just tanned, he was bronzed. He didn't need a cap to make him look good. *He* made the *cap* look good.

Chrissy caught her reflection in the small mirror the other waitresses kept by the kitchen door. She wished she could say the same for herself. These days she didn't make anything look good. She wondered if Reno would even recognize her if he saw her again.

Reno had known her when she still glimmered with her carefully applied Vegas look. Back then, she'd worried about whether her nail polish matched the dress she was wearing that night. She had regular manicures and pedicures and facials. She worried about the bristles in the brush she used to apply just the right shade of blush to just the right area on her cheekbones.

She always looked as much like a fashion model as an ordinary woman could.

At Pete's Diner, she'd stopped wearing blush. The heat from the kitchen gave her cheeks more than enough color. As for nail polish, she'd given up worrying about what color would even go with the fluorescent-orange uniforms Pete insisted his waitresses wear, and so she left her nails unpolished. Instead of a facial, she was lucky to get a good session of soap and water before Justin woke up.

Now she used lip balm instead of lipstick and kept her hair pulled back. In short, she was a fashion disaster and couldn't muster up enough energy to even care much about the fact.

She'd actually debated dyeing her hair to match her natural color and letting it grow back brown just because it would be so much easier to take care of that way.

Funny how having a baby can change what is important, Chrissy thought as she picked up a salad order for table number eleven. She'd applied for the job at Pete's because it was close to her mother's house and she could use her breaks to walk home to nurse Justin. She hadn't even cringed at the neon-orange uniforms. She'd have worn a chicken suit if it meant she'd be close to her baby.

Besides, she'd never liked the flash of Vegas all that much. Her whole time in Las Vegas had been spent trying to be the woman Jared wanted her to be. Not that Chrissy blamed Jared. She knew a man liked to have a glamorous woman on his arm, and she had been determined to please Jared. She'd never been a natural beauty, so she knew she had to work at looking good. She'd spent hours at cosmetic counters talking about the latest eye shadows and lip liners.

Now she didn't have time to do what it took to be fashionable. It was enough if her slip didn't show. The important people in her life—her baby and her mother—cared more about her smile than her makeup, anyway.

Chrissy's mother had been more supportive throughout Chrissy's pregnancy than Chrissy had dared to hope. Chrissy knew from the moment she knew she was pregnant that telling her mother about the baby would be harder than telling Jared.

Chrissy had been a problem to her mother since the day Chrissy was conceived. She was in the first grade when she first heard the word *illegitimate.* She couldn't even pronounce the word, and she had no idea what it meant. When she asked her mother about it, her mother had told her it meant Chrissy was a special gift from God and that she shouldn't worry about that word.

The next month her mother had decided they should move.

Until Chrissy was thirteen, she and her mother had moved almost every year. It was small town to small town to small town. In each town her mother talked about going to the church there, but they never did. Chrissy didn't know how old she was when she sensed her mother was actually afraid of churches.

Finally her mother decided they'd move back to the Los Angeles area. Big cities, her mother told her, were more forgiving of unmarried mothers on welfare.

In Los Angeles her mother found the courage to go to a church she'd gone to many years ago, and she was happy. She repeatedly invited Chrissy to come to church with her.

Chrissy had refused. She'd finally figured out that her mother had been afraid of churches because of the way people had treated her when she was pregnant with Chrissy. Her mother might be ready to forgive church people, but Chrissy wasn't.

The closest she'd been to a church recently was the time she'd walked up the steps of the church in Dry Creek looking for a place to sit while she waited for the café to open one morning.

Ah, Dry Creek.

Dry Creek had occupied her mind since she'd left there last fall. She supposed it was unfair to fantasize that the place was her real home, but she did nonetheless.

For some reason, Pete's Diner had reminded her of Dry Creek. With its worn vinyl booths and fluorescent lights, it looked as solid as the café in Dry Creek. The diner sat squarely between two retirement homes and it had a loyal group of customers. Business here would never be bustling, but it was steady.

When she got the job, Chrissy felt she'd finally landed on her feet. Her mother could stop worrying about her. Chrissy didn't need to ask to know the worries that were going through her mother's mind. Her mother didn't want her to be a welfare mother. She didn't want Chrissy to have to accept the pity of others because she needed their charity. So the job at Pete's was important. It showed she could take care of herself and Justin.

And then two minutes ago, one of the other waitresses had told Chrissy that Pete wanted to see her in his office.

Don't think it's bad news, Chrissy told herself as she knocked on the door outside the office. Just because she'd been caught in the rush of layoffs at other restaurants lately, it was no reason to panic. There had to be a dozen reasons that Pete might want to talk to her. Maybe the fry cook had told him it had been her idea to offer a shaker of salt substitute on the table along with the regular salt and pepper.

"Come in."

Pete was probably grateful that she was concerned about his customers' health, Chrissy told herself as she took a deep breath.

"Please sit," Pete said as he looked up from some papers. Pete had been a semipro football player before he bought the diner thirty years ago and, even with the gray hairs on his balding head, Chrissy thought he still looked as if he would be more comfortable on a football field than behind a desk.

"You wanted to see me?" Chrissy sat down on the folding chair opposite Pete's desk.

Pete nodded and then swallowed. He opened his mouth and then closed it again.

"Is it about the salt substitute?" Chrissy asked. She couldn't stand the silence. Please, let it be the salt substitute. "I haven't heard any customers complain. Except for Mr. Jenkins. But he thought it was sugar and put it in his tea."

"Oh, yes, the salt substitute." Pete looked relieved. "It's never too early to pay attention to good health. I should have thought of offering a salt substitute years ago. Someone mentioned it to the dietitian at the retirement home down the street, and she recommended us to some of the residents who'd never been here before."

"So business is good." Chrissy was starting to feel better.

"It's never been better. That's sort of what I wanted to talk to you about. You see, I—"

Chrissy's cell phone chose this moment to ring. She told herself to ignore it. But she'd gotten the phone only so that Mrs. Velarde could call her. Mrs. Velarde lived across the street from Chrissy's mother and was baby-sitting little Justin temporarily. Chrissy was having as much trouble keeping baby-sitters as she was keeping jobs. She knew the call was about Justin.

"Excuse me," Chrissy said finally as she reached around to unclip the phone from her belt. "I need to get this."

She turned her shoulder slightly and said a low hello into the cell phone.

"There's a man," Mrs. Velarde almost shrieked into the cell phone. "You told me to watch out for a man prowling around, and he's here!"

"Jared's there?" Chrissy was shocked. When she had warned Mrs. Velarde to watch out for Jared, she had never expected him to make the drive down from Las Vegas to see Justin. The bond that had held her and Jared together in high school was no longer even a thread.

Jared had learned that money could buy friends since he'd gotten access to his trust fund, and he no longer needed Chrissy. With his new friends, his life had unraveled even further in the months since Chrissy had left him. He'd told her he was glad she was gone, because now he could date women who really knew how to party.

Chrissy had told him that he was a fool and she was sorry he was the father of her baby.

No matter how isolated Chrissy had felt in high school, she had never turned to the drug crowd for friends. Jared was using drugs, and he had made it very clear he wasn't interested in being a husband and or a father.

But as much as Jared wanted to avoid the baby, Jared's mother was adamant in her desire to know more about Justin. She had given up on Jared ever entering the family business, but she obviously had hopes she could start over and train a baby to be a more obedient heir. So far Jared had refused to tell his mother that Justin was his son, but if Mrs. Bard offered Jared enough money, he might decide to confirm what his mother already suspected and help her try to claim custody of Justin. "You're sure it's him?"

"Well, I don't know what Jared looks like, but there's a man parked in front of my house who keeps looking over at your house. He even went up and rang the bell once, but no one answered, of course, with you and your mom both at work."

"You're sure he isn't a deliveryman or something?"

"There's no uniform. Besides, he's young and good-looking. No one else comes to your house who is young and good-looking."

"I guess it could be Jared. Or someone else his mother has hired."

Mrs. Bard made Chrissy nervous. Mrs. Velarde had already told her that a private investigator had been asking questions about Chrissy in the neighborhood. It had to be someone working for Jared's mother.

"You want me to call the police?" Mrs. Velarde asked.

"He hasn't done anything yet, has he?"

"He sits out there."

"Does he look like someone on drugs?"

"No. He just sits."

"That's probably not Jared, then. Maybe he's a salesman and will go away in a minute or two. Just keep Justin inside until I get home."

Mrs. Velarde grunted. "I'll keep my baseball bat by the door, too. Nobody comes to see our Justin without his mama here."

"Call if you need me." Chrissy said goodbye and flipped her cell phone shut before she saw the concerned frown on Pete's face.

"Trouble at home?" Pete asked.

Chrissy didn't bother to deny it. He knew that much already. And the trouble would only get worse. Mrs. Velarde was scheduled to leave for Florida next week to move in with her daughter, and so far Chrissy had not found someone else to take care of Justin while she worked.

"My neighbor who is watching Justin is worried. I may need to leave for a few minutes and go home if she calls again."

"You're welcome to use the delivery car to drive home. Take as much time as you need." Pete rubbed his hands over his head. "I've never been able to offer the best salaries in the business, but I've always tried to be flexible."

"I appreciate that."

"I've always looked at the staff as family, which is why it's so hard to—"

Chrissy wanted to put her hands over her ears. She

didn't want to hear what was coming next. "But business has been good."

"Business has never been better," Pete agreed. "And your idea with the salt substitute is one of the reasons."

Chrissy decided she didn't need her hands over her ears after all. Maybe the reason Pete had called her into his office was to thank her for the suggestion.

"It was a simple idea," Chrissy said.

Pete nodded. "But it has made all the difference. That's why I wanted you to be the first to know the news."

Chrissy felt a sudden unease. A thank-you would be nice, but it wasn't actually news. "Are we changing the menu again?"

Pete chuckled. "I don't think I'd live long enough to do that even if I weren't moving to Arizona."

"What?"

Pete winced. "I didn't mean to just blurt it out like that. I never was any good at things like this. Actually, I wanted to thank you. The extra business we have because of the salt substitute must be what finally made the diner look attractive enough to find a buyer. A real estate agent called me last week."

"I see."

"The offer is just too good to turn down."

"Will the new owner keep the place a diner?"

"They're thinking along the lines of a tea shop. Crumpets. Scones. That kind of thing."

"I see."

"They've promised they'll have a job for every one of my staff. I wouldn't sell otherwise."

Chrissy started to breathe again. She'd already lost two waitress jobs because business was bad; she didn't want to lose another because business was good. "Do the others know?"

"I'm going to tell them when the shift changes at three this afternoon. That way, everyone will be here."

Chrissy heard a bell in the kitchen. "That must be my last order. I better get out there."

Pete nodded.

For the next hour Chrissy was too busy with hamburgers and chicken strips to worry. And then she got a second call from Mrs. Velarde.

"I've got to go," she said to Pete as she walked to the door of the diner.

He nodded and tossed her a set of keys. "Take the delivery car."

Reno decided everything he had ever heard about crime in Los Angeles was true. Here he was in broad daylight, parked in a residential area, and it sounded as if a dozen police sirens were all going off at once. It had been enough to wake him up from his nap, and he was tired enough to sleep through an earthquake.

Tonight he'd check in to a hotel by the ocean and get a good night's sleep before he left to go back.

He'd pulled into Los Angeles early this morning and had gone directly to the office of Joseph Price, Esquire. Reno didn't know why he'd decided to visit the lawyer. Maybe he just wanted to be sure Chrissy hadn't already accepted the offer before he went to the trouble of trying to find her with the address he had.

He hadn't been in the lawyer's office five minutes before Reno regretted stopping. Chrissy was no match for the man, and Reno would have been happier not knowing that fact.

Reno's distrust of the man only deepened when the lawyer talked about the educational opportunities Mrs. Bard was hoping to give Chrissy's baby.

"She's prepared to pay the costs for a private education, from military boarding school to graduate school at Princeton or Yale—she's even got her eye on some kind of exclusive kindergarten for the gifted in Boston," the attorney said as he offered Reno coffee in a china cup.

"No, thanks," Reno said. "I thought Mrs. Bard lived in Los Angeles. Is she moving to Boston?"

"She doesn't need to move to Boston." The attorney set the cup of coffee on his own desk. "Fortunately, the school is a live-in situation. Twenty-four-hour care and mental stimulation. The baby will grow up to be a genius."

Reno grunted. "Even a genius needs a home."

The attorney took a sip of coffee. "The Bards own

a house in San Marino and another in Vail. The boy won't lack for a place to visit during his school breaks. And there'll be adequate supervisory care.''

Reno didn't like the sound of this. What kind of grandmother was this woman? ''It takes more than a house to make a home. Isn't Mrs. Bard going to bake him cookies?''

The lawyer laughed. ''Mrs. Bard doesn't bake anything. She's a very busy woman.''

''Too busy for a little boy?''

''Don't worry. Mrs. Bard is hoping to make the boy her heir. That should tell you how she feels. Her only concern is that the baby is Jared's son. That's why she hired our firm. She's paying us a handsome bonus if the baby is Jared's son, so of course, we're hoping it is.''

The lawyer started to lift the cup again.

''How much of a bonus?'' Reno asked.

The attorney stopped with his cup halfway up in the air and looked at Reno. ''You certainly ask a lot of questions. Why are you so worried about this baby, if you've never even seen him?''

Reno smiled slightly. He could see the lawyer was beginning to think that Reno might really be the father of Chrissy's baby. It was the first time in the conversation that the question had even seemed to arise. ''Let's just say I want to make sure everyone is happy.''

The lawyer studied the cup he held in his hand. ''I

see. Well, I can assure you Mrs. Bard will want to share her happiness with everyone if we prove to her the baby is Jared's son. So if she's happy, we're happy. Of course—'' he paused ''—if someone else had reason to believe he could be the baby's father, we would want to make him happy, too.''

"You'd pay me off?"

The lawyer shrugged. "I didn't say that, now, did I? I'm just pointing out that there's no way to really prove who the father is without a blood test, and Miss Hamilton refuses to agree to that. I'm afraid Chrissy is both stubborn and foolish. She refused to list Jared on the birth certificate or even to say he's the father, so she can't press for child support. At her age, with only a high school education, she'll never be able to support the baby herself, not working as a waitress like she does.''

"But—" Reno started to protest.

The lawyer waved his hand. "Oh, I have to admit she's a gutsy young woman. She bounced back real fast when she lost her last two jobs. But how much longer can she move from job to job? It might be okay now that she's living in her mother's house, but how long will that last? She won't find a decent place to rent in Los Angeles on her salary. And that's just now. She'll certainly never be able to afford private schools and college. We're really doing her a favor to help her recognize that the baby is better off with Mrs. Bard. It'll save Miss Hamilton years of hard work and heartache. Mrs. Bard is even willing to pay her enough so that she can go to college herself and make something of her life.''

''She *has* made something of her life.'' Reno stood up to leave. ''She has the baby to prove it.''

Reno left the lawyer's office with a sour taste in his mouth and drove to the west side of Los Angeles. The lawyer had at least confirmed Chrissy's current address. After Reno knocked at the house's door and no one answered, he went back to the car to wait. It was hard to get comfortable in the compact space of Mrs. Hargrove's car, but he managed. His waiting had turned to napping when the sirens penetrated his sleep.

Reno saw the woman open her door and wave a baseball bat at him at the same time that the police cars came around all the street corners and headed straight for him.

Reno woke up all the way. People in Los Angeles sure knew how to get a man's attention.

''Come out of your car with your hands up,'' the loudspeaker on top of one police car blared out as the cars pulled to a halt and turned off their sirens.

Reno counted four police cars blocking him in.

Reno hadn't trained a half-wolf dog without learning when to move easy. He put his hands up in plain view and nudged the car door open with his elbow. He couldn't even guess what law he'd broken. Maybe people didn't park in front of houses in Los Angeles, especially not in rusted-out cars with red plastic balls on their antennas. Mrs. Hargrove had put the red ball on the antenna one winter when the snow was particularly high, and she hadn't bothered to take it off.

"I can move the car if you want," Reno called out as he shouldered the door open and stepped out. "And that red ball, it's just a plastic thing from some gas station."

"Keep your hands where we can see them," the voice on the loudspeaker demanded. Apparently the police in Los Angeles took their parking tickets seriously.

Chrissy's heart stopped when she saw the police cars parked in front of her place. Four cars! Whoever was in that car must have tried to take Justin. That was the only thing that would make them send four cars. She knew Mrs. Bard had hired an attorney to try to take Justin away from her, and Chrissy had begun to wonder if Jared's mother would try kidnapping the baby if she got frustrated enough.

Chrissy knew Mrs. Bard could offer her baby all of the advantages money could buy. Sometimes Chrissy felt selfish for even refusing to consider the woman's offer—until she remembered that Jared had had those same advantages, and look how unhappy his childhood had been.

Chrissy pulled her car up behind a police car and got out to rap on its window.

"What's happening?" she asked.

The policeman inside looked up from the report he was writing and rolled down the window. "What do you think you're doing? Keep your head down. He could be armed. Get back to your car and wait."

Chrissy saw the police put handcuffs on some man standing beside an old car. They were all on Mrs. Velarde's lawn. Chrissy could see only the back of the man the police had cuffed. It wasn't Jared, but the man did look familiar. Mrs. Bard must have hired one of Jared's friends.

"I'm not going back. My son's inside that house." Chrissy pointed to the house where Mrs. Velarde lived. Chrissy thought she could hear Justin's cry from here. She was glad to see that the baby-sitter had drawn the drapes to the house.

As Chrissy checked the house she saw Mrs. Velarde standing on the porch with the baseball bat in her hand. She had a housedress on, and her hair was in curlers.

"Go back inside!" Chrissy shouted.

Even though she was watching Mrs. Velarde on the porch, Chrissy also saw the man who was being handcuffed turn at the sound of her shout and look over at her. It was enough to make her eyes turn from the sitter.

Oh, no! Chrissy looked at the man in astonishment. He had a cap on his head that hid his face from the sun, but she didn't need to see his face to know the man who stood there was the last man on earth she wanted to see. Or, rather, it was the last man who would want to see *her*.

She hadn't realized until she'd been seeing her physician for a while that spurts of idiotic tears were perfectly normal for a pregnant woman. She'd never cried before in her life, but when she was pregnant, she'd cried over everything, even dinner invitations from handsome men that she couldn't accept.

"What's he doing here?" Chrissy whispered.

"Dealing drugs, we think," the policeman answered from inside the car. "Or maybe just using them. We don't know."

"Reno Redfern?"

The policeman nodded. "That's what he said his name is. I'm running his plates now to check it out. Do you know him?"

Ten minutes later Chrissy poured Reno a cup of coffee in Mrs. Velarde's kitchen.

"I'm so sorry," the baby-sitter repeated as she wiped her hands on her apron. There were open cardboard boxes sitting in the kitchen with pots and pans in them.

"It's my fault," Chrissy said. "If I hadn't been so paranoid about Jared showing up, I wouldn't have kept asking Mrs. Velarde to keep an eye out for a man on drugs."

Chrissy tried to ignore the boxes. What was she

going to do with Justin when Mrs. Velarde moved to Florida?

"Well, I guess most people don't park in front of your house and then go to sleep," Reno offered.

"I thought you were out on some overdose," Mrs. Velarde admitted as she drew a circle around her head with her finger to signify "crazy."

Reno took another gulp of his coffee. "No harm done. I'm glad you're suspicious of strange men hanging around." He turned to Chrissy. "I don't know if you're aware that Jared's mother has hired a lawyer to investigate you."

Chrissy nodded miserably. "Don't tell me she sent someone to Dry Creek, too."

Dry Creek was the one place that she'd felt was beyond Mrs. Bard's reach. Not a day had gone by since Chrissy left Dry Creek that she hadn't thought about that little town. She'd go to sleep at night with the picture of it in her mind. She'd even made up a little lullaby about the town that she sang to Justin.

Chrissy looked up from her hands. "I'm a good mother, you know. I might be young, but I love my son and we're going to do just fine."

Chrissy knew she'd never give up her rights to Justin. She didn't know much about rashes and formulas. She didn't make much money, but she'd find a way to avoid welfare. Maybe someday she could save enough to buy a small restaurant. She'd be a respectable member of the community. Justin wouldn't regret that she hadn't given him to his grandmother to raise. Besides, she knew how to make Justin smile, and she intended to devote her life to seeing that he was happy.

Reno nodded. As it turned out, he hadn't needed to worry about what to say to Chrissy when he met her. The police had sort of taken care of that. But he couldn't seem to get the conversation into position so he could ask her about moving to Dry Creek.

"It sure looks like you have everything under control." Reno nodded his head in the direction of Mrs. Velarde. "You've got someone to take care of Justin if you want to go out to dinner after work—" Reno swallowed. Now, why had he mentioned dinner? That had nothing to do with moving to Dry Creek.

"Work!" Chrissy set down her glass of water and looked at Reno. "I've got to run. But I'll be back— my shift ends in two hours. Can you stay till then?"

Reno nodded. He'd driven over a thousand miles. He needed to ask the question. "I could even take you out to dinner when you get back."

Reno saw the surprise in Chrissy's eyes. He couldn't tell if it was a good surprise or a bad surprise.

"Oh, there is no need to eat in a strange place," Mrs. Velarde offered. "I'm making meatball soup."

Chrissy left Mrs. Velarde's kitchen before the tears could start. Reno had asked her to dinner again. Of course, this time it might not be a date as much as it was a way for him to find something to eat in a strange city, but it still made her want to cry. She wondered why that was. The doctor hadn't said the tendency to tears would continue after Justin was born.

Chapter Four

When Chrissy got home, Mrs. Velarde announced that the soup was not enough for dinner. "Better you should go out to eat with Reno. A nice man like him, he needs a full meal. Maybe some fish. I'll watch the baby until your mother gets home."

Chrissy didn't like to rely on her mother for child care. Her mother had made enough sacrifices all her life for Chrissy.

"Mom's working late tonight," Chrissy finally said. "Some last-minute meeting. I should take Justin with us."

"Nonsense." Mrs. Velarde shooed her out of the kitchen and into the living room, where Reno stood holding Justin. "The baby will be more comfortable here. Mr. Reno—he has been so kind, playing with the little one and cutting the onions for the soup so I don't cry the onion tears. And me—I almost had him arrested. Now he must eat.''

Mrs. Velarde stopped to beam up at Reno.

''But I'm not even dressed for dinner.'' Chrissy looked down at the orange uniform she still wore. Pete had the eye of a football player, and he believed a uniform should be seen from a distance. The orange dress was obviously not something to wear on a date—if Reno was in fact asking her out on a date, and not just looking for someone to guide him to a good restaurant.

''You look fine,'' Reno said as he handed Justin to Mrs. Velarde. ''I hear there's a great seafood place at the end of Mullen Drive. Matt's Galley. Mrs. Velarde said it's a favorite of yours.''

Chrissy knew enough about men to know that they would at least look at a woman before saying she looked fine if they were heading out on a date. Well, she supposed that was her clue. This wasn't a date. They were just two people who were hungry for seafood.

''How was work today?'' Reno asked.

Chrissy noticed the candle at the table cast shadows on Reno's face, but it did nothing to dim the startling blue of his eyes.

''They're going to turn the diner into a tea shop.'' Pete's announcement had been hard for most of the staff. Some of the waitresses had worked for Pete for ten years or more. "But Pete assures us we'll all have jobs with the new owners."

Chrissy found it hard to concentrate on talking about her job.

She wondered if Reno could be any better looking. Back in Dry Creek when she'd been out at the ranch, Reno's good looks just sort of matched the scenery. The sky had stretched from east to west with nothing but the Big Sheep Mountains to stop it from reaching down to level ground. The ground itself had been golden with fall colors. Even the air had smelled rich with the promise of moisture. Reno's good looks had just blended into the countryside, and no one seemed to particularly notice them any more than they noticed the sky or the mountains.

But here…Chrissy knew it was unusual for three different waitresses to ask if they needed more water within the space of five minutes. It was clear that Reno was getting plenty of notice. Not that he seemed to be paying any attention. Chrissy was glad he wasn't, even if this *wasn't* a date.

The waitresses at Matt's Galley wore snappy shorts and black nylons, which made Chrissy feel even more dowdy in her orange dress. The dress didn't even fit properly, since it was a size too big. She'd bought the uniform secondhand from one of the other waitresses rather than buy a new one of her own. Tonight she wished she'd spent the extra twenty dollars.

Reno frowned. "Mrs. Velarde told me you've lost a lot of jobs—"

Chrissy flushed. "The restaurant business can be unpredictable." The two restaurants she'd worked for before Pete's had both gone out of business.

"All I meant was—well, when she told me that, I wondered if Mrs. Bard's attorney was behind it."

Chrissy was amazed that the thought hadn't occurred to her. "Would he do that?"

Could he do that? Chrissy asked herself. The first restaurant had closed after they lost most of their business to a sandwich truck that parked outside their doors and practically gave away gourmet sandwiches to anyone who wanted one.

The next restaurant had been closed when someone left a lit candle on a table near the stack of folded napkins.

"But one of the restaurants burned down— wouldn't he lose his law license doing things like that?" Chrissy protested. "I've never met the man, but he can't be that foolish."

"I *have* met the man," Reno said, "and I think he'll do whatever he can to collect the bonus Mrs. Bard is offering. I have the impression the amount is very generous. And all he really has to do is convince you Justin is better off with Mrs. Bard than you. He's talking Princeton and Yale. And I'm sure he's not breaking any laws personally. He probably knows people who arrange things."

"Justin would never be better off with someone else." Chrissy grabbed hold of the only thing she could in the swirling thoughts around her. How could she compete with Princeton and Yale? She'd be lucky to afford community college. Still… "I'm his mother and I love him. I'll never let him go."

Reno hadn't realized he was holding his breath until he felt the tension slowly leave his body. He was glad Chrissy sounded so adamant. "Then you'll need to come back to Dry Creek with me."

"What?"

Reno frowned. He hadn't meant to say it so bluntly. He hadn't shown a glimmer of the charm Mrs. Hargrove thought he'd shown in first grade. "That is, if you want to come."

Chrissy was still looking startled.

"We have free sundaes in the café on Friday nights," Reno added. He swore the temperature inside the restaurant had just risen twenty degrees. "They have eleven kinds of toppings."

"No one has eleven kinds of toppings."

"They count the sprinkles and the nuts."

There was silence for a moment, and Reno began to think the impossible was happening.

"I don't accept charity," Chrissy said.

"It's only a sundae." Reno told himself he shouldn't be disappointed. He hadn't really expected her to agree.

"I mean coming back to Dry Creek. I don't need anyone's pity. Justin and I will do fine."

"What's pity got to do with anything? It's an invitation."

Reno remembered Mrs. Hargrove's advice to be charming, so he did his best. He relaxed his frown and smiled with all his heart.

Chrissy blinked. Reno should warn a woman before he smiled like that. His smile made her lose her place in her thoughts, and she had a feeling she needed to think. "From you? Is the invitation from you? Are you asking me to come?"

"Well, yes."

Chrissy felt as if she'd fallen down a rabbit hole. Reno was sitting there and asking her to—to what? Had he seen her looking at him and admiring his eyes? Was he suggesting she move back to Dry Creek so they could live together? Or was her mother right? Chrissy's mother had cautioned her that men would think she was more—what was the word her mother used— *available* because of Justin. Chrissy hadn't believed her. But here sat Reno, with a heart-stopping smile on his face, asking her to move back to Dry Creek.

"Babies are a lot of work. I don't have much time for fun."

"I know what you mean," Reno said. He looked relieved that she had changed the subject. "I have a dozen or so calves that eat up a storm. I don't get

much done except feeding them this time of year—
and I need to get to the plowing if the mud ever dries
up.''

"What I meant is, I don't go out like I did before
Justin was born.''

Reno wasn't looking as distressed as Chrissy
thought he should be if he was getting her message.

"I'm not going to have sex again unless I'm married.'' Chrissy finally decided she might as well be
blunt. "So there's no reason to ask me to come live
with you.''

"Oh,'' The surprise on Reno's face couldn't have
been anything but genuine.

"Oh.'' Chrissy echoed. She wondered if she could
hide under the table in her orange dress or if it was
hopeless. "You weren't asking me that, were you?''

"I never thought you would—'' Reno took a deep
breath. "I mean, not that if I had thought you
would—I'd—of course, I'd not—''

"Would you two like more water?'' a cheerful
blond waitress inquired as she stepped closer to the
table.

Chrissy said, "Yes.''

At the same time Reno said, "No.''

The waitress glanced at Reno's face and hesitated.
"I'll come back.''

Chrissy didn't blame the waitress. She would have
run away, too.

"I never would suggest that you come live with

me in that way.'' Reno said the words slowly. Chrissy only had to look into his eyes to know he was sincere. ''Of course, you probably know that I find you attractive, so it's not that I wouldn't want to—''

''Really?'' Chrissy was feeling better already. So Reno found her attractive.

''I asked you out,'' Reno said indignantly. ''You were the one who refused.''

''I was pregnant.''

''Pregnant women eat.''

''So you thought I needed help and you decided to ask me to move to Dry Creek?''

Reno nodded.

''Well, I still don't need your charity.'' Chrissy crossed her arms. She'd already thought about moving back to Dry Creek, and she'd gone over in her mind any possible jobs. There were none that she could see.

''Who mentioned charity? I'm offering you help.''

''I don't take handouts. I need a job to support myself and Justin.''

''Mrs. Hargrove thought you could stay with her.''

Chrissy blinked. ''Mrs. Hargrove? Does she know about Justin?''

Reno nodded. ''She's the one who started this idea.''

''Mrs. Hargrove wants me to move there and stay with her?'' Chrissy had liked Mrs. Hargrove when she met the older woman at Thanksgiving dinner at the

Redfern Ranch. But Mrs. Hargrove was clearly a churchwoman, and Chrissy had always thought churchwomen looked down on unmarried mothers. She knew they had looked down on her mother years ago. "And she knows about Justin? Isn't she worried that I don't have a husband?"

"Not that she's mentioned."

"Why?" Chrissy crossed her arms. "Why would she want me to come stay with her when you and I both know she has to think I'm one of those sinners?"

Reno smiled. "Mrs. Hargrove teaches first-grade Sunday school. She thinks everyone is a sinner."

"Well, if she thinks that, then why—"

Reno interrupted her softly. "She also knows about forgiveness and grace. She knows life isn't always easy."

Chrissy relaxed her arms. Maybe there were people like Mrs. Hargrove who weren't set on judging her. "Well, if I had a job—"

"We'll worry about a job when we get there."

Chrissy's cell phone rang. She kept the phone clipped to her waitress uniform, so it was still in place. Chrissy reached down to unhook the phone, and she put it to her ear. "Hello?"

"There's a fire!" Mrs. Velarde said breathlessly. "I called the fire department, but it's still burning."

"Grab Justin and get out of the house!" Chrissy stood up from the table.

"Not my house," Mrs. Velarde said, and then she took a deep breath.

Chrissy relaxed. "Just stay inside, then, until the fire department gets there."

"It's your mother's house," Mrs. Velarde continued.

Chrissy turned to Reno.

Reno had already stood and laid three twenties on the table. "Let's go."

As Reno drove faster than he should down the street toward her mother's house Chrissy reminded herself that her mother was working late. *Please, let her be working late,* Chrissy added, and realized in surprise that it was the first time in her life that she could remember praying. It must be all this talking with Reno. She hoped Mrs. Hargrove's God was listening to her.

The sharp, hot smell of burning wood grew stronger as Reno drove the car to the fire truck parked in front of Chrissy's mother's house.

"Was anyone inside?" Chrissy called out to a fireman before Reno had pulled the car to a stop.

The fireman shook his head. "Didn't look like it."

Chrissy slumped against the car seat. "If she had been there, she could have died."

"They would have gotten her out."

"I need to go to Dry Creek with you," Chrissy said softly. "If he will set fire to my mother's house, he will do anything. My mother's not safe with me here, and neither is Justin.''

''I'm sure they'd never hurt Justin.''

Chrissy grimaced. ''I know. All they want to do to him is take him away from me.''

Chrissy turned at the sound of another car driving down their street much too fast. The car braked and her mother stepped out and started running toward the house. ''Chrissy!''

''I'm over here, Mom,'' Chrissy called from the car window.

Then she stepped out of the car and into her mother's arms.

Reno watched Chrissy hug her mother. So Chrissy was coming back to Dry Creek with him. He wished it hadn't taken a fire to make her decide. It sure hadn't been his charm that had swayed her in the direction of Dry Creek. Still, he'd feel better knowing she and Justin would be where he could keep an eye on them. Strangers would be easy to spot in Dry Creek.

Reno remembered the interstate that ran past the Dry Creek exit and frowned. A car could pull into the town at night and no one would notice. Chrissy and Justin would be a lot safer at the Redfern Ranch than in Dry Creek. His dog, Hunter, would frighten off any trouble from the city. Maybe once he got Chrissy and Justin to Dry Creek he could mention the safety of the ranch.

Chapter Five

The smell of burned wood and rubber hung in the air as Chrissy put a box into the trunk of Mrs. Hargrove's car. The car was parked in the Velarde driveway, and Chrissy's mother was inside at the Velarde kitchen table. Most of what Chrissy owned had been burned in the fire, so Mrs. Velarde had given her a cardboard box to pack what was left. Quite a few of Justin's things were all right, because they had been with him at the Velardé house.

The only other things that Chrissy still owned for herself were several sequin-dresses from her days as a cocktail waitress in Las Vegas. She'd given the dresses to Mrs. Velarde to keep for the Salvation Army truck when it came by for donations. Now she'd need to wear them sometimes, even if it was only when she had her orange waitress uniform in the washing machine.

The small box fit into the trunk beside the spare tire. It wasn't much to start a life with, and Chrissy was glad Reno had sounded as if he felt she could find a job. If she had a job, she could buy some more clothes and a few toys for Justin.

Her mother had surprised Chrissy by urging her to move to Dry Creek.

"The Lord knows you're used to moving. I'd feel better knowing the two of you are safe," Chrissy's mother said as she looked over at Reno and smiled slightly. "Besides, I'll know you're with family there, and that makes me feel better."

Reno frowned. "We're not really related. Just by marriage. We're not cousins."

Chrissy's mother smiled more broadly. "Oh, I know that. I meant Garrett. He'll be there, won't he?"

"Oh, yeah, in a few days."

Chrissy's mother nodded. "Chrissy has always been fond of Garrett. Besides, I may be able to move up there, too, when I wrap things up here with the fire."

Chrissy had told the fire captain about her suspicions, and he had written everything down, even Mrs. Bard's full name and Jared's phone number. The captain said the fire looked as if it had started on the outside wall by the garage. There was nothing electrical around, and although they wouldn't know for sure until they did some testing, he thought the fire had been started with gasoline. Of course, he added, whoever set it was probably only intending to scare Chrissy and her mother and not actually burn the house down. If someone had been home, they would have smelled the smoke long before the house burned.

The streetlights made shadows on the asphalt, and Chrissy was glad Reno had agreed to leave tonight for Dry Creek. She got nervous every time a car drove down the street. Would that lawyer send someone to see if she was still there?

Once, a black sedan stopped at the end of the street, and she didn't relax until she heard the music being turned up loud. It was some old sixties music that she hadn't heard for a long time. She recognized some Beatles songs and a Carpenters song. Then she heard the Mrs. Robinson song. It was odd music for teen-agers, but who else would turn the music up like that? The black sedan wasn't a kid car, but it might belong to one of their fathers.

Chrissy shook her head. She wasn't used to feeling spooked, and the more miles she put between herself and Los Angeles, the better she'd feel.

"You'll call Pete's and explain?" Chrissy reminded her mother. Ordinarily, Chrissy wouldn't leave a job without giving notice, but she knew Pete would be relieved to have one less employee to worry about in the sale of the diner.

Chrissy's mother nodded. "And you call when you

get to Dry Creek. I'll be staying with Mrs. Velarde for a few days.''

It was past midnight before Chrissy strapped Justin into his infant seat and crawled into the back seat herself. ''Let me know if you want me to drive.''

''Maybe you can get some sleep.'' Reno came around the side of the car with a blanket and handed it to her.

''I'm happy to help drive.'' Chrissy hugged the blanket to her. It smelled of peppermint, and she couldn't wait to snuggle into its warmth. ''You haven't had any sleep either.''

''I had a nap this afternoon with Justin.'' Reno slid into the driver's seat and checked the mirrors. He frowned a minute and then opened the car door again. Standing outside, he twisted the red ball off the antenna. ''This car is odd enough, but with that red thing sticking up like that, a blind man could follow us to Dry Creek.''

Chrissy fell asleep before Reno got on Interstate 15. He noticed her stir at the first sound of Justin's crying at dawn. There was desert on both sides of the car and a string of cars behind them on the single-lane highway.

''Do you want to stop in Vegas? We're coming up on the city.'' Reno looked back at Chrissy and held his breath. It had occurred to him somewhere around Barstow that Chrissy might want to stop in Vegas and stay there with Jared or at least visit him and show him their baby. Reno knew she'd said she wasn't returning to Jared, but sometimes people didn't know what they wanted until it was in front of them.

"If you don't mind," Chrissy said sleepily. "Any gas station will do. I should nurse Justin."

Reno started to breathe again. "No problem."

The casinos of Vegas stood straight ahead on the road like giant cartoon buildings. In the gathering dawn they looked almost eerie with their flashing lights. Reno pulled into the next gas station that he saw also had a pay phone.

He'd decided to call Mrs. Hargrove so she could post a sign in the café asking for someone to work as her housekeeper. As proud as Chrissy was, she wouldn't accept a job that she thought was created just for her. A sign on the bulletin board in the café when she got there should convince her that Mrs. Hargrove's job was legitimate. Chrissy wouldn't need to know Reno was the one paying her salary.

Chrissy sat in the back seat of the car while Reno made his phone call. She was glad he'd decided he had some things to do so that she could nurse Justin in private. She loved these moments with Justin, even though being this close to Las Vegas made her nervous. When Justin was satisfied, she rearranged her blouse and looked around.

Chrissy rolled down the car window and glanced at the other cars in the gas station. Was it her imagination, or could she hear the same songs that she'd heard when she packed up earlier to leave with Reno? Yes, there it was—the faint sound of the Mrs. Robinson song.

She looked around more closely. None of the cars at the pumps looked familiar. Besides, the music was probably from a CD, and there could be millions of copies of the song. She looked over the cars at the pump again. She didn't see a black sedan, and that's what had been in her neighborhood.

Chrissy was glad when she saw Reno walking toward the car. He'd gone into the minimart and was carrying a white bag and two cartons.

"I got us some milk and donuts." Reno slid the items through the open window and into Chrissy's waiting hands.

"Thanks. What do I owe you?"

"Don't worry about it."

"I can pay." Chrissy had about thirty dollars in her purse. Her mother was going to send the check from Pete that would cover the hours Chrissy had worked this week. "I might need to owe for the gas, but I can pay for the food as we go."

"You don't need to pay for the gas. I was coming this way anyway."

Chrissy couldn't think of any reason Reno would drive to Los Angeles. When she'd visited him on his ranch, he'd made a point of telling her that he never traveled.

"I don't take charity," Chrissy reminded him, reaching into her purse and pulling out two dollar bills. "Here."

"I'm not that poor." Reno frowned at her in the rearview mirror as he started the car. "I can pay for everything."

If Chrissy had been looking around instead of arguing with Reno, she would have noticed that the music she'd heard had gotten a little louder, and that a black sedan pulled out from the other side of the minimart before backing up so it was no longer in view.

"We'll split the cost of the gas," Chrissy finally said. "I'll pay you back when I get my check."

Reno grunted in response as he drove the car out of the gas station area.

"You never did say what brought you to Los Angeles," Chrissy said a few minutes later. Surely he hadn't driven that far just to give her a ride back to Dry Creek. Of course not. He hadn't even known she would want to move back there.

"I went to see the ocean."

"Oh, and did you like it?"

"I don't know yet."

"You mean you didn't stop and see it?"

Reno shrugged. "I'm young. I've got lots of years to go see the ocean."

"I wish I'd known that's why you came. I could

have stayed in Los Angeles another day if you wanted to go to the beach.''

''It's all right.''

Chrissy shifted in the back seat. ''It would have been fun to show you the ocean. We could have gone to the pier and ridden the old carousel.''

''I bet Justin will like that in a few years.''

Chrissy tried to ignore the picture forming in her mind of her and Reno and Justin going on a beach vacation. That was something that would never happen. He hadn't even said that. She knew Reno was being kind. But by the time Justin was old enough to ride a carousel, Reno would have grown tired of befriending a single mother. That was another lesson she had learned from her mother's past. The occasional man who had wanted to date her mother was usually not interested in being an instant father, and so he hadn't lasted long as a friend to her mother, either.

Chrissy could tell the difference in the air as soon as they drove into Montana. Justin was sleeping, and the inside of the car was peaceful. They came into the state on Interstate 15 and turned off on Interstate 90 at Butte to head east.

The farming area smelled fertile with rain and wild grass. Clouds gathered ahead of them when they passed the downtown area of Miles City and began the last miles leading to Dry Creek.

Chrissy felt her whole body relax as she watched

the space around her. Now, why had she never noticed how little space there was in Los Angeles? Everywhere you looked in L.A. something stopped you from seeing very far. But here in Montana nothing stopped a person's gaze except for the Rocky Mountains to the northwest and the gentle slopes of the mountains to the east that she knew were called the Big Sheep Mountains.

"Are there any sheep?" Chrissy asked. "In the mountains."

"Not for years since the cattle took over," Reno replied as he made the turn off the interstate to go into Dry Creek.

Chrissy took a deep breath. She was really going back. She hoped Reno hadn't exaggerated the welcome she would receive. She kept pushing her nervousness to the back of her mind, since it was too late to turn back anyway. "Are there a lot of cattle in Dry Creek?"

"More cattle than people." He paused. "I hope that doesn't bother you."

"Bother me? Why would it bother me?"

"Some women might find Dry Creek lacking in excitement after life in the big city."

"Oh, look—" Chrissy pointed to the curve in the road. The gravel road widened a little at that point. Instead of snowbanks there was wild grass on the edge of the road, but Chrissy recognized the place anyway. "That's where we met."

She blushed. That hadn't come out right. "I mean the night when your truck broke down—"

"—and you gave me a ride." Reno finished the sentence for her as he slowed to a stop. "I remember. That was some night."

Chrissy remembered that night, too. If she hadn't been so angry, she never would have decided to drive her cousin's truck to Dry Creek, even though Garrett had left the keys with her and given her a couple of lessons on how to shift the gears on the sixteen-wheel truck. But the minute she'd discovered Jared with another woman—in the most "with someone" sense possible—she hadn't been able to stay in Las Vegas.

Her instincts had told her to go to Dry Creek to find her cousin, and that was all she'd wanted to do. "When I was in trouble, I always looked for Garrett."

"He's a good man."

Chrissy wondered if Reno even knew that it wasn't Garrett who had eased her pain on that trip. Reno had given her all the sympathy she needed, until by the time she left Dry Creek last fall, she'd realized she didn't need so much sympathy after all.

That night they met, she had managed to drive the truck fine on the interstate, but once Chrissy had turned off on the gravel road into Dry Creek, the truck started to cough. She'd never seen a night as dark as that cloudless, moonless one.

She'd been half spooked by the lights of a stalled truck ahead, but also half relieved. Maybe the other driver could tell her what to do about that coughing in the motor.

Chrissy had pulled the truck as far to the shoulder of the road as she could before she'd opened the door and climbed down from the cab. She'd left Vegas in such a hurry that she hadn't changed her dress or grabbed a coat. She was still wearing the short glittery white dress that Jared had picked out as her wedding dress.

The night air had been cold enough that her arms were covered with goose bumps. Her hair, bleached a champagne blond to please Jared and curled to sweep away from her face, had lost any sense of fashion around Salt Lake City and become so windblown that it looked as if she'd taken a fan to it instead of a curling iron.

At first Chrissy had thought the other truck was deserted and her heart sank. Then she'd seen the long denim-clad legs lying on the ground under the truck's engine. When the rest of Reno slowly crawled out from under the truck, she'd stopped in her tracks.

She had expected to meet a short, stocky farmer with thinning hair who would be shy and happy to help her. Instead, she'd seen a guy who should be plastered on every month of some hunk-of-the-year calendar, and her heart had sunk even further. Good-looking men, in her experience, really didn't even try to be as helpful as plain-looking ones.

Bringing herself back to the present, Chrissy

glanced up at Reno in the mirror. She had to admit that he was confusing for a good-looking guy. He didn't act as if he was superior. And he had certainly been helpful to her. "I'm usually not as crazy as I was that night."

"I thought you were an angel," Reno said simply.

Chrissy glanced up again and saw Reno looking back at her. Since she was in the back seat to be close to Justin, she and Reno had carried on long conversations through the mirror for two days now. Chrissy kind of liked the flirtatious way it made her feel.

"It was dark out."

Reno grinned. "And you sparkled with all that glitter on your dress. It was an honest mistake. I didn't think to check for wings."

"Not many angels pull up in a sixteen-wheeler truck."

"They do when your own truck is dead and it's cold enough outside to freeze your toes off." Reno paused. "I never thought of it, but I owe you for the ride that night."

"Of course you don't owe me," Chrissy said a little more sharply than she'd intended. Justin moved in his sleep and lifted his fist up to his mouth.

"You keep saying you owe me for this trip we're taking right now. If you owe me for *this* ride, then I owe you for *that* ride."

"It's not the same," Chrissy said softly.

"You might have saved my life. It was cold

enough that night for a man to freeze to death. So I owe you for more than just the ride. I owe you for— preventive medical services.''

''You would have found a way to keep warm.''

Chrissy blushed. She suddenly remembered the way Reno had kept them warm that night. He'd wrapped blankets around them both individually and then wrapped himself and his blankets spoon-fashion around her on the small bed in the back of the cab of her cousin's truck. Chrissy couldn't ever remember feeling so warm and safe.

''Well, I'm willing to call it even between us if you are,'' Reno said. ''I won't pay you for that trip and you won't pay me for this one.''

''I can't pay you anyway until I get my check or find a job,'' Chrissy pointed out as she reached over to rub Justin's back. He was starting to wake up, and she liked him to know she was there. ''So until then we can call it even.''

Reno grunted as he turned the car's wheel to the right. ''We'll call it even—period. I don't want you giving your wages to me.''

As Reno made the wide turn, Chrissy saw the small town of Dry Creek come into view in the distance. ''We're almost there.''

The sky was partially cloudy, but there was no wind. She could tell because someone had white sheets hanging on a clothesline and they did not move. The snow flurries that had covered Dry Creek most of the time she was here last were gone. In their place were broad stretches of mud. Someone had put wooden planks around so people could walk without stepping in the puddles. She noticed two extra-wide planks in front of Mrs. Hargrove's house. No doubt someone had put them there so the older woman would be able to walk more easily.

The planks were an act of kindness that touched Chrissy. Dry Creek wasn't a dressed-up town like Las Vegas, but the people here cared about each other. Chrissy wondered if they could care about her and Justin, as well.

She didn't want the trip to end. She'd been comfortable thinking about going to Dry Creek, but she wasn't so sure she was comfortable actually arriving here.

Reno had entertained her with stories of what had been happening in Dry Creek since she'd been there last. She learned about his new calves and Mrs. Hargrove's arthritis that was sometimes so bad she couldn't peel potatoes. He told her about Lester dressing up as Elvis on April Fools' day and the Friday sundae night at the café.

He even told her about going to church again and what that had meant to him. He talked about forgiving his mother for leaving the family all those years ago. He told her he'd never quite understood about grace when he'd been a young boy, but now that he was a man he felt humbled by it. He wasn't so much forgiving his mother, he said, as trying to see her as she was, the way God might see her.

Chrissy didn't quite understand what he was saying, but she couldn't doubt his sincerity.

For the first time ever, Chrissy began to wonder if God could be real. She'd had people talk to her about God before, but never with the matter-of-fact directness Reno had. He talked of God as naturally as he would the sky or the mountains. Chrissy knew beyond a doubt that God was real for him, because Reno didn't make a big deal of trying to convince her of anything. Reno talked about God with the same warmth he used when he talked about Mrs. Hargrove or his sister, Nicki.

As Reno was telling her about the different things that were happening, he'd pass along greetings to her from various people in Dry Creek. He said that Elmer had asked him to tell her he'd buy her a cup of coffee when she came to town. And Linda from the café had asked Reno to tell her she was looking forward to Chrissy coming to town.

During all the days when they talked, Reno had not indicated anyone had a negative thought about her coming to the area. But Dry Creek was a small, conservative town. She was sure she'd find her share of turned shoulders and unwilling welcomes. It had been just eighteen years since her mother had had a bad experience in a small town because she was an unmarried mother, and eighteen years wasn't that long ago.

"I should comb my hair," Chrissy said. As she recalled, churchwomen were big on combed hair. "Or roll it into a bun or something."

"Your hair looks fine," Reno said.

"You're right. It's this orange dress they'll think is strange. No one wears an orange dress this bright. They'll think I'm nuts."

"They know about the fire. Nobody cares what you're wearing. Besides, Linda wears those kinds of colors all the time."

Chrissy reached for her purse anyway. A touch of light lipstick couldn't hurt.

"We're here." Reno slowed the car to a crawl. "We might as well get something to eat at the café."

Chrissy forced herself to look out the windows of the car and take a deep breath. The people of this town had been friendly to her when she'd been here last fall. If the fact that since then she'd had a baby without the benefit of marriage made any of them treat her any differently, then they were the losers, not her.

"There's not as many houses as I remember." Chrissy forced herself to concentrate. She could do this. "The town's smaller than I thought."

"Yeah," Reno said curtly. "One café. One store. Seventeen houses. Seventeen and a half, if you count the Andersons' basement. One church. That's it. No growth expected. Not even a post office.''

Chrissy lifted her head. She'd taken on bigger challenges and done fine.

Reno watched Chrissy get ready to face Dry Creek and his heart sank. She looked as if she was getting ready to walk the plank. Was it really that bad to live in a small town like Dry Creek? ''It's not like you'll need to be here forever.''

''Huh?''

''I mean, the lawyer is going to give up sooner or later. Then you can move back to Las Vegas.''

''Oh.''

''Or L.A. if that's where you want to go,'' Reno said as he parked the car in front of the café and took the keys out of the ignition.

''But I don't have a job in L.A. anymore.'' Chrissy reached over to unbuckle Justin from his car seat.

Speaking of jobs reminded Reno that he hadn't called Mrs. Hargrove since he'd talked to her when they stopped in Las Vegas. He hoped she had remembered to put a notice on the bulletin board in the café asking for a live-in housekeeper.

Reno opened the back door for Chrissy. ''Here, let me hold Justin while you get out. And he'll need a blanket. It's a little chilly out here.'' Reno had held Justin many times over the past couple of days, but he continued to be surprised every time Chrissy handed him the baby at how small Justin really was.

This time was no exception. Chrissy had assured Reno several times that Justin was a healthy weight for his young age, but Reno still wanted Dr. Norris to check Justin out.

"Remember, if you take a job, you need to ask for this Thursday off so we can take Justin to the doctor in Miles City."

"I can't ask for a day off the first week of the job." Chrissy stepped out of the car and stretched. "We'll have to postpone the doctor's visit until the next week."

"Well, we'll wait and see." Reno didn't say that Mrs. Hargrove wouldn't care what day Chrissy took off. After all, he wasn't supposed to know about the job that was posted inside on the bulletin board.

"He sure is an agreeable little guy," Reno said as he looked down at the baby. "Look at him smiling."

"Babies that young don't smile. Its just gas. It says so in the baby books."

"Those books don't know everything. I can tell by the look in his eyes that he's smiling at me." Reno hated to give the baby back to Chrissy. It suddenly hit him that this was probably the last time he would get to hold the little one. "He knows I'm the one who taught him how to make a fist."

"I think that's pretty natural. So he can suck his thumb."

"Yeah, but I showed him how to hold his fingers

so he can get a good grip on a baseball when he's older.''

Chrissy smiled as she held out her arms for Justin. ''He'll appreciate that.''

Reno gave the baby to her. ''If you ever need someone to watch him, let me know.''

Reno figured he was due some visitation rights. After all, he'd changed Justin's diapers several times on the road. That should give him *some* rights.

''Thanks. I'll remember that.''

Chrissy squared her shoulders as she cradled Justin to her. Reno figured she was preparing herself to face Dry Creek. He only hoped she would give the place a chance.

Chapter Six

Chrissy stepped through the door that Reno held open for her and entered the Dry Creek Café with her baby cradled in her arms. She took a deep breath. It was midmorning and she'd made it home. She remembered the smell of baking biscuits and coffee from when she'd been here before. And the black-and-white checked floor had been in her dreams on more than one night. Six or seven tables were scattered around the café like before.

But something was different. Three tables were pushed next to the large window overlooking the street. Lace half curtains covered the bottom of the large window and matched the white tablecloths covering each of the three tables. In the place where bottles of ketchup sat on the other tables, silver vases stood filled with pink silk flowers. Matching pink napkins were placed beside the silverware on those tables. A wide aisle separated the three tables from the rest of the more casual ones.

Chrissy nodded. That was clever. It made the place feel as if had two restaurants instead of just one.

"Linda thinks we need more class," Reno said as he turned to leave the café again. "I'm going to bring in the diaper bag in case you need anything. I'll be right back."

A delighted shriek made Chrissy look toward the door that led to the kitchen, and she saw Linda stand still for a moment in the open doorway before she came rushing toward her. "You're here!"

Chrissy felt her heart smile. It sounded as if she had one friend in Dry Creek besides Reno. With the two of them by her side, she'd be fine.

"Oh, I can't wait to see the baby!" Linda whispered as she stopped about a yard from Chrissy and then tiptoed closer. Linda had a butterfly tattoo above one eye and a copper-red streak in her dark hair. "Is it sleeping?"

"No, he's awake."

"So it's a boy."

Chrissy nodded. She decided she had no reason to feel self-conscious about her orange dress here. Linda was wearing a purple velvet dress and a large pink apron.

Linda just stood grinning at her. "And you! How are you? You know, I meant to write, but I lost your address and then I forgot to ask Garrett for it again and, well—" She stopped to take a breath. "You're here!"

"It's good to be back," Chrissy said. "I thought about writing you, too, but there was the baby and then I was working and—well, it's good to see you."

Chrissy knew Linda and her boyfriend, Duane "Jazz" Edison, were running the café to earn enough money to buy a farm of their own so they could get married. Unless Linda had had a birthday since Chrissy was here last, Linda was twenty.

"Now, sit down and tell me about the baby," Linda said as she motioned to one of the tables with the flowers on them. "What does he like to do? Are you nursing him or is he on the bottle? I want to know everything. I love babies."

The door to the café opened again, and Reno came in with the diaper bag.

"Well, Justin eats good, so he'll be growing fast," Chrissy reported.

"He's going to be a baseball player someday," Reno added as he set the diaper bag on the floor at Chrissy's feet. "He's got a good grip in his fingers. Don't you, big fella?"

Chrissy watched as Reno ran his thumb softly over the smooth skin on Justin's tiny hand. "I can feel him practicing his pitches already."

Justin gurgled in response to Reno's words.

"That's right," Reno murmured.

Chrissy's throat went dry and she had to swallow. Where had she been for these past days? She hoped Justin wasn't becoming too attached to Reno. Was it possible for a baby to even do that? Chrissy remembered how painful it had been for her when she was young and her mother's boyfriends would leave. The first few times it happened, Chrissy didn't understand and thought the men had disliked her for some reason. She didn't want Justin to have that same hurt in his life.

"The baby seems to like you," Linda said quietly to Reno.

"Yeah." Reno grinned as though he'd been given a first-prize ribbon.

"Justin just likes the sound of men's voices," Chrissy added quickly. She was beginning to see just how complicated this all was.

She had more to worry about than whether Justin was becoming attached to the sight of Reno. She also had to worry about the hurt Justin could do to Reno.

Reno might not recognize the speculative look in Linda's eyes, but Chrissy did. Linda was wondering if Reno was Justin's father. Of all the things Chrissy had worried about in coming to Dry Creek, this was one that hadn't occurred to her. Reno had told her about the letter that had come to the Dry Creek postmaster, but she didn't believe anyone in Dry Creek would seriously believe Reno was the father of her baby.

"The baby's father is still in Las Vegas, you know." Chrissy would rather talk about almost anything than Jared, but she wanted the record to be straight in this small town. If she had to talk about her past with someone here, she'd rather it was Linda than anyone else.

"That's got to be hard," Linda said as she reached over to give Chrissy's shoulder a squeeze. "So it was the guy you were engaged to…"

Chrissy nodded. "But it's all right. We'll be fine, Justin and I. Just as soon as I get a job."

"Oh, that's right." Linda jumped up. "Getting a job won't be a problem in Dry Creek. We have a bulletin board over here for jobs."

"Really?" Chrissy asked as she turned to Reno. "Will you hold Justin for a little bit while I look at the ads?"

Reno nodded as he put out his arms and accepted the baby.

If he hadn't been distracted by Justin, Reno would have noticed right away that something was odd. As it was, it took a few minutes of the excited chatter over at the bulletin board before it dawned on him that Mrs. Hargrove's posting for a housekeeper wouldn't generate that much enthusiasm.

Reno stood up and walked closer to the bulletin board that was on the west wall of the café. He couldn't believe his eyes. There had to be a dozen notices scribbled on index cards and tacked to the board.

"Here's one that looks interesting," Chrissy was saying. "Dancing instructor wanted for gentleman. Twenty dollars an hour."

Linda nodded. "Jacob put that up. He said he was thinking he'd like to be able to dance the next time someone has a wedding in that barn south of town."

"We did line dancing at that wedding," Reno interrupted. "There's nothing to learn. You just put your foot where the caller tells you to put it. In. Out. Whatever."

"Before you got there, we had waltzing," Linda said.

"I can waltz." Chrissy was still running her fingers down the cards lined up on the board. "Here's one that calls for someone to do some mending."

"Elmer swears he's got a dozen shirts with no buttons on them," Linda said. "He said he's flexible on the timing of it, too. He's lived without buttons for a while now. He just wears a sweater over everything. But with summer coming, he wanted some shirts to wear that don't require a sweater."

Reno looked at the cards in astonishment. Had everyone in town listed a job on the board? It sure looked like it. What were they doing? Everyone knew there were no jobs in Dry Creek.

"Ah, here's one for a cook/housekeeper," Chrissy said. "That sounds promising."

Reno relaxed. Finally she was looking at Mrs. Hargrove's notice.

"But where's the Wilkerson place?"

"Lester's?" Reno's voice came out so loud it made Justin start to fuss. Without thinking, Reno started to slightly rock the baby where he stood.

"Now, now." Chrissy turned and started to coo. "It's all right."

Reno wasn't sure if Chrissy was cooing at him or Justin. "Why's Lester advertising for a cook?"

"Well, he is alone out on his ranch all the time. He could probably use some help," Linda said as she gave Reno a look that said he shouldn't be making this so difficult.

Reno grunted, but didn't back down. "The man eats from cans. All he does is heat it up. Hash. Chili. Soup. It's all the same. A cook would be wasted on him."

"I don't know," Chrissy said thoughtfully as she held out her arms for Justin. "He did seem to enjoy that pie at the big Thanksgiving dinner at the ranch last fall. I make a pretty good apple pie, and I think that's his favorite."

Reno frowned as he handed Justin to her. He didn't like the thought of Chrissy making pies for Lester. "If he wants pie, he can come to the café."

"We don't serve pie," Linda reminded him.

"And it's a live-in position," Chrissy said as she cradled Justin upright against her breast. "That way

I wouldn't have to pay rent anywhere, and Justin will have a place to play.''

''Justin can't even walk yet. It'll be a good six months before he needs a place to play,'' Reno protested, and then thought a minute. ''How long do you plan to work for Lester, anyway?''

Chrissy leaned in to see the card better. ''I don't know. It doesn't say what the salary is. All it gives is a number to call.''

''I'll call him,'' Linda offered as she walked toward the kitchen. ''You just keep looking.''

''There's got to be a better job there,'' Reno said as he started to scan the notices to find Mrs. Hargrove's. ''Something closer to town.''

''I don't mind being out of town.''

''You say that now. But the wind blows something fierce out there on the ranches. And the solitude. Some days you don't see another soul. Just horses, with a few chickens thrown in for excitement.''

''Well, I'd see Lester,'' Chrissy reminded him as she rocked Justin against herself. ''Three times a day at least for meals.''

Reno ground his teeth. ''Lester doesn't talk much, though. You'd be bored in no time. He doesn't have a television. He doesn't get any magazines except for the *Farm Journal*.''

Linda opened the door from the kitchen and came back into the room. ''The job pays eighty-five dollars a week and room and board.''

"That's not enough," Reno said firmly as he went up close to the board and scanned the notices. When he found the one he was looking for, he put his finger right next to it. "There. That's the job for you. A housekeeper for Mrs. Hargrove. Room and board included."

Chrissy walked over to look up at the small, neatly penned notice that Mrs. Hargrove had tacked to the board. She Chrissy shifted Justin in her arms so she could read the announcement better. "But her job only pays seventy-five dollars a week plus room and board."

"I'll pay the extra ten," Reno said. Lester must have read Mrs. Hargrove's notice and decided to out-bid her. "That way you won't lose money by working for Mrs. Hargrove."

Chrissy tipped her head up at him suspiciously. "Why would you do that?"

"Yeah, why would you do that?" Linda asked along with Chrissy.

"Ah." Reno ran his hands over his hair. He was guessing Mrs. Hargrove hadn't told Linda about their plan. "Because Mrs. Hargrove is an older lady and she needs the help more than Lester does."

Reno hoped Mrs. Hargrove never heard about this conversation. She didn't think of herself as old, and she'd snap at anyone who implied she was not able to take care of herself.

Chrissy was still looking at him funny.

"And I know Mrs. Hargrove can't afford to pay you any more herself because she's on Social Security, so I want to help." Reno smiled. "She's been good to me, and I want to do something for her."

"I noticed the other day that her porch needs fixing," Linda offered.

"Thanks. I'll go take a look at it." Reno gritted his teeth. Whose side was Linda on? "I should have checked the porch myself before I headed down to Los Angeles. Those old boards usually have problems about now."

"She said you usually do it and don't take any money for it," Linda said.

"In the past we've settled it with her giving me a plate of her homemade chocolate chip cookies."

"Well, of course, if all she has is Social Security, she can't afford to pay anyone," Chrissy said thoughtfully. "I wouldn't feel right taking any money from her, and I don't need cookies. I'm sure I can help her with what she needs when I'm not working at Lester's."

"But you can't work at Lester's," Reno said. He could see the question in Chrissy's eyes and knew it was on the tip of Linda's tongue. He needed to focus. Ah, he had it. "He's a single man, and it wouldn't be proper for you to live in the same house with him alone."

Chrissy's face turned red. "I hope you're not suggesting I would do anything but bake pies for the man.''

''No, I didn't mean that at all.'' It had to be about sixty degrees inside the café. There was no reason for Reno to be sweating. ''I just mean you have to think of Justin.''

''I'm perfectly capable of taking care of Justin,'' Chrissy said coolly.

''Besides, you're talking about Lester,'' Linda said as though he'd suggested Chrissy was willing to date a troll.

Reno bowed his head in defeat. ''I'll pay you a hundred dollars a week plus room and board to work at the Redfern Ranch.''

''Doing what?''

''Well, I like pies, too—and there's the house.''

''You don't need a housekeeper. I can't take a job that's just charity.''

''I have the calves to feed.'' Reno looked up and thanked God silently. Yes! That was it. ''The poor things need someone to take care of them, and I'll have to start plowing any day now. Who's going to take care of them?''

''Don't they have their mothers to take care of them?'' Chrissy didn't look convinced.

''Not these calves,'' Reno said mournfully. ''They're all alone in the world. No mother. No father.''

Reno hoped his prize bull forgave him although it

was true that the animal had never shown any interest in his offspring, so the calves actually had no father when it came to having someone care for them.

"Oh, the poor things," Chrissy whispered as she glanced down at Justin, who was sleeping in her arms. "It's bad enough not having a father, but not having a mother, too, would be just awful."

Chrissy broke off with a stricken look at Reno. "I'm sorry, I forgot about your mother."

Reno stopped the triumphant war whoop that wanted to come rushing out of his mouth and he managed to wince instead. "It is hard. Not everyone understands."

"Of course they don't," Chrissy said soothingly.

"So you'll take on the feeding of the calves?"

"Well, I suppose it is more important than baking pies for Lester," she agreed. "Although his would have been more convenient, since it was room and board."

"My job includes room and board, too," Reno offered.

"Oh, no, you convinced me that wouldn't be proper."

"Oh, it's different with Reno," Linda said smoothly. Reno thanked her with a smile until she added, "Mrs. Hargrove was saying that he admitted in the post office the other day that he feels only family feelings for you on account of the fact that you're almost cousins."

"Almost cousins?" Chrissy asked faintly.

Reno could see Chrissy was surprised. He was shocked himself. "I don't remember saying anything quite like that."

"Oh, well, Mrs. Hargrove goes for the essence of what a person says," Linda said with a wave of her hand. "You know how it is—sometimes you're not even sure what you mean, and then Mrs. Hargrove sums it up for you and it's right on the nose."

"I see." Chrissy swallowed. "Well, I've never had an almost cousin before…"

"What about Garrett? He's your cousin," Linda said as she adjusted the salt and pepper shakers on a nearby table. "Just pretend Reno is Garrett."

"I could do that, I guess," Chrissy said.

Reno frowned. He didn't like the fact that Chrissy could make a promise like that so easily. He sure couldn't promise to see her through the eyes of a cousin any day soon.

"I don't see why you're looking for a job anyway," Linda said as she moved to another table and swung out a chair for Chrissy to sit down. "If that guy in Vegas is the baby's father, shouldn't he be paying enough child support to take care of you both? I thought you said he had a trust fund or something."

"He does," Chrissy said as she sat in the chair. "But it's complicated. To get child support, I need to claim he's the father, and if I do that, I'm worried

Jared's mother will have a better case to get custody.''

''But you're the mother. She can't just take your baby away from you.''

''She's already got some attorney trying to find out things about me so he can say I'm an unfit mother.''

''And if that doesn't work, he's trying to scare her into giving up Justin,'' Reno added. ''Someone set fire to Chrissy's mother's house just before we left L.A.''

''You're kidding?'' Linda said as she looked from Reno to Chrissy. ''Some lawyer would do that?''

Reno nodded. ''He might not do anything himself, but he'd pay people to cause some damage.''

''Wow.'' Linda frowned. ''He's serious. I thought he was just some kind of crazy guy who wrote letters to stir up trouble.''

''I still have the letter,'' Reno said as he patted his shirt pocket. ''I'm keeping it in case we want to get a restraining order on him or something.''

''It's not the lawyer I'm worried about—it's the people he hires that scare me,'' Chrissy said. ''I'm glad Justin isn't old enough to walk or crawl. I'd be a nervous wreck every time he went out to play.''

''Oh, surely the lawyer will give up after a while. He can't care that much,'' Linda said.

''It's Jared's mother who cares. And she never gives up. Oh—'' Chrissy stopped in surprise and turned toward Reno. ''I never thought about that—

that's why you didn't want me to take the job at Lester's and stay at his place, since he's not married. You were worried Mrs. Bard might use it against me in a custody battle.''

Reno grunted. He should have thought of that. ''You can never be too careful.''

''Well, you don't need to worry about Mrs. Bard when you're in Dry Creek,'' Linda said firmly. ''We'll take care of you and Justin. We keep an eye out for strangers.'' Linda paused. ''Well, except for a few times when things have gotten out of hand.''

Reno grimaced. He could tell from the look on Linda's face that she was remembering the time a stranger had come to Dry Creek and dressed up as Santa Claus so he could get close enough to the woman who was playing the angel in the church Christmas pageant to try to shoot her. Come to think of it, Linda had felt sorry for the man in the Santa Claus costume and given him a free spaghetti dinner from the café before the pageant.

Linda looked at Reno. ''I guess she'd be better off out at your ranch.''

Reno nodded. ''My dog, Hunter, doesn't let strangers get too close unless I give him the all-clear sign.''

And I'll be there, Reno thought. He remembered that what had saved the angel was that Pastor Matthew had risked his life to save hers. Even Reno had been touched by their story of love and happiness.

''I don't really think the lawyer would send someone up here. Do you?'' Chrissy asked as she looked from Reno to Linda. Justin seemed to sense his mother's fear, and started to fuss.

''Of course not,'' Reno said quickly as he scowled at Linda.

''You're perfectly safe here,'' Linda added when Reno finished.

''It's just that I keep hearing that music playing in my head,'' Chrissy said as she put Justin to her shoulder and looked over at Reno. ''Remember after the fire, there was that black car with a few guys in it, and they were playing those old songs from the sixties—it sounded like a CD or something. I remember because they were playing that song—how does it go…the Mrs. something one—''

''Mrs. Robinson?'' Linda asked as she stood up from the table. ''I don't believe it. They've called here.''

''Who?'' Chrissy asked as she started patting Justin on his back.

''Some guy called asking how to get to Dry Creek, and he had that music playing in the background. I think he was on a cell phone—we don't always get good reception here if someone is on a cell. Usually we don't even get the call, but sometimes it comes through and sounds faint like this one.''

''They called here?'' Chrissy looked over at Reno.

Linda nodded. ''We finally got the phone for the café listed under Dry Creek Café, Dry Creek, Montana. We thought we should ask for reservations for our new dinner section." Linda motioned to the three tables in front of the window. "I'm so sorry. We never would have gotten a listing if we'd known."

"Did he say where he was when he called?" Reno walked over to the window and looked out at the road leading into Dry Creek. He saw a puff of dust in the distance, but it looked like a pickup.

"He asked for directions from Salt Lake City," Linda said, and then looked over at Chrissy. "And I invited him to try the café while he was in town. He said they would, so he must have someone with him."

"We should call the police," Chrissy said, and then bit her lip. She stopped patting Justin on the back, and he started to cry. "Of course we can't do that. No one's done anything. It's not a crime to play sixties music."

"We'll tell our deputy sheriff anyway. He can keep an eye out for strangers," Reno said as he held his arms out to take Justin. "And we'll tell the men at the hardware store. Not much gets by Elmer and Jacob."

Chrissy gave the baby to Reno, and she stood up and started to pace.

"You're safe here," Linda said. "We have a neighborhood watch program going—well, not the official thing, but we watch who comes and goes. Not that there're many strangers anyway."

"I do feel safer here than in Los Angeles," Chrissy admitted. It made sense that there would be fewer strangers here and fewer chances for mischief. "My nerves just need to settle down."

Chrissy stopped pacing at the window. She could see the Dry Creek church across the street, and the Big Sheep Mountains were in the distance. The Montana landscape didn't offer many places for a criminal to hide. She should feel safe here.

Then she glanced over at Reno. He was rubbing Justin's back.

Maybe she was relaxing too soon. The lawyer wasn't the only man she needed to worry about while she was here.

Chapter Seven

Reno was just about as content as a man could be. The midday sun was shining in the café window with enough force that it might even be drying up some of the mud outside. If it did, Reno would have an easy drive to the ranch.

Not that mud was on his mind too much. Chrissy was sitting across the table from him, and she had a happy flush on her face. They had both just eaten a couple of the best hamburgers Reno had ever tasted.

Life didn't get any better than this, Reno decided as he leaned back in his chair.

Everyone had calmed down after Linda decided that maybe the man who had called on the phone was Jacob's nephew, who was planning to visit the old man in a couple of days and be there for Jacob's big birthday party.

"I'd forgotten he might call," Linda said again as she held Justin up and smiled at him. "Pastor Matthew told me they wanted to have a birthday party at the Elktons' barn and asked us to provide the food, so of course Jacob's nephew had this number."

"If you need help with the party, let me know," Chrissy said before she took one of the last French fries from her plate and dipped it in ketchup. "I can help you handle a hungry crowd."

"Oh, that's a relief," Linda said. "I wasn't sure how I was going to manage everyone, even though we're going to have a limited menu. Grilled steaks and baked potatoes mostly, since that's Jacob's favorite dinner. Besides, it's a good menu for cowboys, and they're inviting the whole crew at the Elkton ranch."

Reno frowned. He wasn't sure he wanted those cowboys to get a close-up look at Chrissy. "Maybe I should help instead. You know how those cowboys are when there's a party."

"I've worked in Vegas," Chrissy said as she picked up the last French fry. "I can handle anything."

"Maybe you can both help," Linda suggested as she laid Justin over her knees and started to rub his back. The baby gurgled in delight. "We'll even be able to pay decent salaries."

"Oh, you don't need to pay me," Chrissy said. "It'll be fun to have a party."

Some of the joy went out of Reno's day. He supposed Chrissy's disappointment in Dry Creek was inevitable, but he didn't like to think about it. "This might not be your usual party. Besides, we don't have parties very often around here, so you wouldn't want to get used to it. Mostly it's a pretty boring place."

"I don't know about that. We've had a lot of weddings in the last year." Linda eyed Reno suspiciously. "I don't know if those are exactly parties, but they have sure been fun. You don't want to sell this place short."

"Well, I guess there have been the weddings," Reno acknowledged. Maybe if he was lucky, there would be another wedding to help keep Chrissy entertained. Women sure liked weddings. He looked over at Linda. "I don't suppose you and Jazz are planning to get married any time soon?"

Linda's smile tightened. "Jazz and I are no longer engaged."

"What?" Chrissy said. "Why didn't you say something? Here we've been chatting away about all my problems and—oh, I'm so sorry."

"Don't be sorry," Linda said. "We just realized we have incompatible goals. It's really for the best that we found it out now, before we went to the trouble of getting married."

"How incompatible can your goals be?" Reno had always pictured Linda and Jazz as a sensible engaged couple who agreed on what they wanted out of life.

"I thought you two were planning to buy the Jenkins place and raise cattle. Isn't that what this café is about? Saving up enough money for that ranch?"

Linda lifted her chin and then bent to rub Justin's back some more. "There's more to a marriage than which piece of land to farm and what cattle to buy."

"Well, of course, but—"

Reno was interrupted by the sound of a loud scraping that came from outside on the porch.

"What's that?" Chrissy said.

Reno could see the shape of a man through the glass on the café door. Something about the shape looked familiar, but it didn't look quite right.

The door opened, and Lester Wilkerson stepped inside the café.

"What's with him?" Reno had never seen Lester in a suit before. He didn't even know the man owned a suit. Yet here he was, wearing a black suit and a tie. He was holding a metal bucket. Lester had slicked his red hair back and shaved his face so close he'd nicked his chin. The metal bucket was dented in a few places and obviously old, but Lester was holding it out in front of him as if it was a grand bouquet.

"What's this?" Reno asked. Now that he'd gotten a closer look at the bucket, he could see it held what looked like a small bush.

"Flowers," Lester announced as he took a deep breath and smiled. "Well, not yet, but Mrs. Hargrove told me there will be some soon—geraniums."

Lester held out the bucket to Chrissy. "I know women really like their flowers and there aren't any blooming in Dry Creek right now because of the rain—well, and winter, of course—but there should be some flowers on this plant soon. They'll be red, according to Mrs. Hargrove." Lester paused as though to remember something Reno figured he had memorized, and then continued after clearing his throat. "The way I see it, if one flower says welcome to a woman, a whole plant should say it ten times better—so welcome to Dry Creek, Chrissy Hamilton."

"Why, thank you," Chrissy said as she accepted the bucket and held it in her lap. "I'm touched."

Reno wasn't touched. He was astonished.

"I know women like them fancy bouquets," Lester continued. "But I figured you might like a plant to keep in the kitchen window. Sort of a homey touch."

Chrissy blinked. "I think that's the sweetest thing anyone has ever done for me."

Reno wondered if she had forgotten he had just driven over two thousand miles to bring her and Justin back to Dry Creek. "Yeah, it's sweet. That's Lester for you. As sweet as they come."

"I just wanted to welcome you to Dry Creek," Lester said again nervously. Now that he didn't have the bucket to hold, he used one hand to smooth back his hair. "I'm sure you and your baby will be happy here. I heard you're thinking of taking the job I posted for a cook—''

''She's not taking the job,'' Reno interrupted. ''She's going to work on the Redfern Ranch bottle-feeding the spare calves.''

Chrissy moved the bush so she could give Lester a soft, apologetic smile. ''It's only because I think family should stick together, and Reno says we're practically cousins.''

Lester grinned. ''Oh, well, that's okay then. I can see why you'd want to help out your cousin. Cousins, huh?''

Lester turned to Reno and winked before turning his smile back to Chrissy. ''And I bet your cousin told you what a good neighbor I am.''

Reno forgot Lester had asked him to put in a good word for him. ''He's the best—but about this cousin business. Actually, it was Mrs. Hargrove who said—''

''Ah, yes, Mrs. Hargrove. Wonderful woman.'' Lester grinned even wider. ''Besides, my place is just next door to the Redfern Ranch. I'll be seeing you almost every day as it is. I usually pick up the mail for both places and bring it out from town.''

Justin was starting to cry. Reno didn't blame him. The little one couldn't see his own mother through all the leaves that went into that plant. Linda moved the baby so he cradled against her shoulder and could see everyone.

Reno frowned as he turned back to Lester. "I thought you stopped getting our mail when Nicki got married. I haven't seen you around, and the mail's always on the counter when I go to town."

"Yeah, well." Lester shrugged. "I've decided I should be more neighborly, so I'm starting up again. The Bible says to do unto others you know."

Reno had never heard Lester quote from the Bible before.

"It also says it isn't good for a man to be alone," Lester added as he dipped his head for a pause. "I used to enjoy those morning visits with Nicki before she got married. She'd always cut me a big piece of her coffee cake and pour me a cup of coffee." Lester managed to look forlorn. "It was more than the food. I kind of miss that womanly touch—being a man on my own isn't easy."

Reno wondered when the violins were going to start.

Chrissy had a sympathetic look on her face.

"Well, you'll have to stop and visit when you bring the mail. I'm not sure I can promise you coffee cake. But it'll be good for you to visit. I'm sure you and Reno have lots to talk about."

"Reno's usually out working in the fields by the time I bring the mail." Lester grinned.

Reno grunted. "I'll make a point to come in and say hi—since you're so lonely and all."

"Now, won't that be nice." Chrissy beamed.

Reno wondered if Chrissy had any idea what Lester was up to.

Chrissy told herself she had never been happier. She was lying in a bed with crisp white sheets that she had put through the ranch's washing machine yesterday and then hung out to dry on the clothesline that had been strung years ago outside the bunkhouse. When she took the sheets off the line late yesterday, they smelled like the outdoors. She'd cuddled in their scent all night. She'd never had a sheet that had been dried outside in the sun before, and she hadn't known what she was missing.

Yes, it was a good life, she said to herself as she opened her eyes and looked around. Speaking of the sun, it was just starting to shine in through the windows she had washed yesterday. She took a deep breath. The air still smelled from the lemon floor polish she'd used on the hardwood floor. Her arms still ached, but her heart was happy.

Justin was in a makeshift crib beside her bed. And they were both in their own home. Well, as close to their own home as she had ever had. Reno had agreed to let her use the bunkhouse as her own while she worked on the Redfern Ranch.

And it was all because of that geranium. Chrissy needed a place to keep the plant, and she didn't want to move a plant in a bucket into someone else's kitchen. And where else could she keep it, since she didn't have a front door to set it beside?

Something about the plant made Chrissy want to have her own place. Granted, the bunkhouse needed some work, but the building was basically sound. She had curtained off the bottom half of the main room to make a private bedroom. Reno had helped her put up a single bed frame and then brought over the mattress from Nicki's old bed.

''You may as well have this single,'' Reno said. ''Nicki and Garrett have a queen bed now in the new house they've built. We've got a spare dresser you can use, too.''

Reno had mentioned earlier that, in addition to building a new house on the knoll about a half mile from the old ranch house, Nicki had also insisted on buying two washing machines and putting one in the ranch house for when she wanted to do any wash over there.

''And maybe I could put up a plank table like the ones we set up for the Thanksgiving dinner last fall,'' Chrissy suggested. She had decided to sign up for as many as possible of the jobs that she had found on the bulletin board at the café. She had already called Elmer and said she'd be happy to sew buttons on his shirts. A table would be useful while she mended.

Reno nodded. ''You can use the rocker from the ranch living room, as well. You'll want that when Justin can't sleep.''

Reno said that as long as he was bringing the rocker over, he might as well bring the television in from the barn, too. The small black-and-white television was one Reno used during calving season, but it would get a strong picture if he hooked the antenna to the roof.

"Don't go to any special trouble," Chrissy said as she moved her plant. She'd set the geranium's bucket inside the front door to the bunkhouse, but then decided maybe it should go by the rocker on the small rug there.

"Oh, I'd do this for any hired hand," Reno said, and Chrissy believed him. "The Redfern Ranch has a reputation to uphold."

Chrissy started to lift the bucket, but Reno stopped her. "You're not supposed to lift anything."

"Why?" Chrissy blushed as she realized why. "Oh, that's before the baby is born. It's okay afterward."

"Still," Reno said as he moved the plant to where she wanted it. "We have a reputation."

"Oh—you mean the ranch's reputation." Chrissy swallowed. "As I remember, your ranch has been here since the turn of the century." The stories Linda had told Chrissy last fall about the ranch's history had been very entertaining. "I'd love to hear more about those days."

The first Redfern had been a young Englishman who had came west and worked on a cattle drive.

After the drive, he bought this ranch in southern Montana and stocked it with Texas longhorns. As the ranch grew, the bunkhouse filled up with a whole assortment of cowboys.

Chrissy was hoping Reno would tell her more stories about the ranch, but he changed the subject to floor wax. Since he didn't have much to say about floor wax either, she decided he must not want to talk about the ranch.

If Chrissy had that kind of a family history, she would be telling stories about her great-grandparents to everyone who would listen.

As it was, she had very little family history. Her mother's parents had died when she was still a baby, and her one uncle, Garrett's father, had never been very friendly toward her and her mother.

Her mother refused to say anything about Chrissy's father other than that he had died in an accident before she was born. The only relative Chrissy had, besides her mother, was her cousin, Garrett.

Oh, well, she told herself as she yawned and stretched in the bed. She'd been on the Redfern Ranch for only a day so far. She could be patient to learn all its stories. In the meantime, it was six o'clock and she should get up and go to the main house to fix Reno breakfast.

Reno had not asked her to make breakfast, but it was her first official day on the job and she wanted to make a good impression. She'd even rinsed her waitress uniform out last night and hung it out on the line so it would be ready for her first day working with the calves.

Chrissy was determined to be a good calf feeder. She hoped the calves weren't afraid of orange. She knew red was upsetting to bulls, and the bright orange of her uniform was a little too close to that color for her own comfort.

But Reno had told her she didn't need to worry. He planned to be with her the first few times she fed the calves to make sure everything went all right.

Chapter Eight

Reno didn't know it was possible to burn instant oatmeal. It wasn't as if he'd never thrown a packet of flakes into a pan of boiling water before. Of course, the other times he'd made oatmeal, he hadn't also attempted to make biscuits, so he had remembered to turn the gas burner off when he put the flakes into the water.

But this morning those biscuits had distracted him. Well, the packet said they were supposed to be scones, but they had looked like biscuits, at least when he put them in the oven.

Oatmeal hadn't seemed enough to feed Chrissy, and he thought eggs and bacon might be too much like plain old ranch food. That's when his eyes had fallen on the packet of scone mix. He wondered when Nicki had bought that packet, but he was thankful she had. He'd decided to fix the scones and a pot of tea in case Chrissy shouldn't be drinking coffee yet on account of Justin.

The scones promised to have dried cranberries and orange peel in them, and they had looked suitably lumpy when Reno dropped them by teaspoon onto a cookie sheet just as the directions said.

He thought the dried cranberries and orange peel would have that civilized touch that would let Chrissy know she wasn't at the earth's end.

How was he to know the gas oven would decide to turn blazing hot? For the past decade that old oven had been taking twice as long to cook meat loaf as the recipe promised it would. Why did it need to change its habits now?

Reno had decided to do all the cooking yesterday when Chrissy asked about using the washing machine. Thankfully, there was a new washing machine in the ranch house because Nicki had just bought one, but that was the only thing in the kitchen that wasn't forty years old.

Reno didn't want Chrissy to discover how hopeless the rest of the kitchen was. Women judged a house by its kitchen. He knew he shouldn't care what Chrissy thought about this old house, but he did. It was his home. He expected to bring his bride here someday. Of course, the bride he would bring would be grateful for an old gas stove, because she would understand the sacrifices a young ranching couple generally had to make.

He didn't feel like explaining all of that to Chrissy, however, and he wouldn't have to if he did all the cooking. Of course, he couldn't expect a city woman to like the kind of bachelor cowboy breakfasts he usually made of fried potatoes with onions and plenty of baking powder biscuits and eggs over easy. But he was willing to try some new recipes.

How hard could cooking for a city woman be anyway? Reno had asked himself yesterday when he made the decision.

He was afraid he was getting the answer this morning.

Reno slid the main window up and propped the door open. The sun was just beginning to top the mountains behind the ranch, and there wasn't so much as a breeze coming through. Reno shook his head in disgust. It was always windy here except on the day when a man wanted to blow the smoke out of his kitchen.

Reno looked out the door at the wood boards on the porch. Yes, they were wet. There had been the usual drizzle of rain last night, and so there would be more mud today.

Reno lifted his eyes to the gray sky that backed the mountains. If he had any doubt that God had a sense of humor, mud would convince him otherwise. But then, Reno had read some of the book of Job already this morning, and he guessed life could be worse. At least Job hadn't mentioned any mud.

Chrissy looked at the mirror in dismay. The bunkhouse bathroom had a long mirror that was so old the surface bulged a little and gave a distorted image. At least, she hoped some of the way she looked was due to distortion in the mirror.

She had made a mistake by leaving her orange dress outside on the clothesline to dry overnight. How was she to know it would rain? Her dress wasn't just wet, it was also cold and stiff. Even when she brought it inside and laid it out by the small wall heater in the room, she knew it wouldn't be dry for breakfast. She'd be lucky if it would be dry by lunch—or dinner, as they called the noon meal here.

She had only three other pieces of clothing in the box she'd brought from Los Angeles. One was a strapless black evening gown that probably didn't fit anymore since she'd had Justin. The next was the white almost-wedding dress that Reno had said made her look like an angel. The third and final choice was a dark blue evening gown that not only had straps, it had a good solid front and back. It might have sequins, but it did look respectable. She had bought the blue gown in Vegas, hoping Jared would like it and she could stop wearing the black one. He didn't like it, but she had kept it anyway.

Chrissy shook her head. It was either the blue gown or her old wedding dress.

It wasn't even the blue gown that was making her look funny in the mirror. She looked more closely. Something was wrong with her complexion. She looked a little yellow around the eyes and green around the mouth. If she hadn't felt so good, she'd have thought she was sick.

Thankfully, she had makeup in her purse. Although she'd been too busy to wear much of it lately, she'd also been too busy to clean out her purse, so she had everything she needed: eyeliner, foundation, lipstick, blush and eye shadow.

Chrissy used the mirror as she put her makeup on, and by the time Justin woke up she decided she looked pretty normal. After all, she wouldn't want to scare the poor calves on her first day as their feeder. And she was sure they'd like the blue dress better than the orange one. And as for Reno, all the men she had ever known liked a woman who was dressed up enough to step off the cover of some magazine. She doubted Reno was any different from Jared when it came to that.

Yes, it's all under control, she told herself as she looked at her watch. It was only six-thirty. Most people didn't eat until seven, so she'd have plenty of time to scramble some eggs and make toast for Reno. It'd be the perfect way to let him know she intended to earn her salary.

* * *

Reno forgot all about the burned scones when Chrissy showed up at the kitchen door with Justin in her arms. He must have missed explaining something to her about working on the ranch. They'd never had a dress code at the Redfern Ranch before—well, unless you counted the fact that every cowboy was required to have a bandanna around his neck if he was riding into dusty territory—but Reno wished he could pull out a sheet of policies related to how a ranch hand should dress.

Chrissy was as pretty as a greeting card. Her brown hair curled up into fluffy blond tips that were tucked behind her ears. Her green-gray eyes looked even more mysterious than he remembered them from yesterday. Her lips shone with a raspberry color he figured was a Vegas special. He could say for sure none of the women in Dry Creek wore a lip gloss like that one, not even Linda.

But it was the dress that stopped him cold.

''You look great,'' Reno said, and swallowed. The dress reminded him of that time just before midnight on a clear night when the stars were all out. It also reminded him of all the reasons that Chrissy didn't belong on the ranch. She was fine china, and most days on the ranch they used paper plates. ''New dress?''

Chrissy winced. ''Not really. It's just that I washed

the orange one last night, and I put it on the line to dry.''

"And it rained,'' Reno finished for her in relief. It wasn't as bad as he feared. "Well, that's easy to fix. I can give you some old shirts or something.''

"I couldn't take your clothes.''

"Oh, I know they'll be big, but we can fix you up with a belt.''

"I mean, I make it a rule never to accept charity. That goes for clothes, too.''

"It's not charity. It's just being practical. I have plenty of work clothes, and you need some.''

Chrissy lifted her chin. "I take care of myself and Justin.''

She walked right past Reno into the kitchen. "Now, I came to fix breakfast for you, since it's my first day on the job.''

Reno was grateful the kitchen was still dark enough that the smoke didn't show. If Chrissy wondered what had been burning, she was too polite to ask about it.

"Oh, I already fixed breakfast for us. You don't need to worry about meals. And before you ask, meals are not charity. They're part of your wages.''

Chrissy nodded. "We had a meal included at the diner when I worked there. That's a nice benefit. Thank you.''

Chrissy hated to admit it, but she was relieved. She realized she might have overstated her cooking abilities just a tiny little bit when she'd talked about her apple pie. She'd been so enthused about getting the job at Lester's, she'd forgotten a few things about that pie.

She'd remembered them yesterday as she was scrubbing the floor. It had been several years ago, and she had bought canned filling and refrigerated pie-crusts from the store. All she'd really had to do was unfold the crust into the pie tin and add the apples from the can. Her mother had even crimped the edges.

Of course, the pie had tasted good, but something told her a rancher would expect her to know how to crimp the piecrust herself. Besides, she didn't see any grocery stores around where she could buy a handy piecrust. People around Dry Creek probably made their own crusts.

Still, she didn't want to take advantage of Reno. "I'd be happy to help with the cooking. Feeding the calves doesn't seem like enough to do if the job includes room and board."

"No, that's fine. Feeding the calves is all you were hired for—you don't want to spend all day working."

"But that's hardly like work at all." Chrissy had gone with Reno yesterday to meet the calves she was to feed. She had noticed that Reno moved through the livestock with comfort, and the calves came running over to him as if he was their mother. Reno rubbed the calves' ears, and Chrissy petted each one individually and assured each one that she would take good care of it.

''Well, you also have to see to Justin.''

''Yes, but that's not my job here. I want to do a good job, too. I need to work to earn my salary.''

Reno had never known a woman so desperate to make sure she earned every penny of her salary. If he hadn't been trying to keep the true state of the kitchen a secret from her, he would happily have let her do the cooking just so he wouldn't have to think up other tasks. But he knew women set great store by kitchens, and he didn't want her to know that nothing worked right in the one he owned.

''You're fixing up the bunkhouse,'' Reno finally said. ''Nicki and I sort of let things go down there, since no one has been living there. That's worth something.''

''But I'm doing that because I live there. I really feel I should do something more.''

Reno had a flash of inspiration. ''You can do the shopping.'' That should be safe. All women liked to shop. ''For the groceries, that is.''

Reno felt as if he'd solved his problem. She'd never realize that the refrigerator in the ranch-house kitchen went clunk in the night or that the gas stove was so old the burners needed to be lit with a match.

Reno didn't know why he wanted to keep the truth of the ranch kitchen from Chrissy, but he did. He supposed some stubborn part of him wanted to think that she might someday decide that it would be all right to live on the ranch.

Of course, he assured himself, he was only trying to prove to himself that his mother could have endured living here in peace if she hadn't left all those years ago. Or maybe that his own bride wouldn't dislike this old kitchen too much when he got married.

"It's very comfortable here in the kitchen," Chrissy said as she sat down at the breakfast table and settled Justin on her lap.

Reno eyed Chrissy suspiciously. She didn't look as if she was being sarcastic, but now that she'd brought it all up, he had to confess. "It's old, but I have plans to replace some of the appliances someday. I have to start with the farm machinery first, before I work on the house."

Reno half expected the look of protest that grew on Chrissy's face.

"Well, you can't get rid of those old appliances. They look like they're from the fifties—they're probably collector pieces by now."

Reno was taken back. He didn't know anyone who would want to collect the old things, unless it was the junk dealer in Miles City. "You're not upset because I said the farm equipment came before the kitchen?"

"No, why should I be?"

Yeah, Reno thought to himself. Why should she be? She was clearly only staying long enough to find the appliances quaint instead of frustrating. "I will admit there's nothing like those old gas stoves for baking bread."

Reno had decided as long as he'd made the kitchen sound old-fashioned, he should continue. And what he said was true. He could still remember his father talking about the bread Reno's grandmother had baked in those old stoves. Reno had always wished she'd been alive when he was born.

Chrissy looked at him. "Were you baking bread this morning?"

"Ah, no," Reno said. "And don't worry about it. I was hoping you like cornflakes with peach slices."

Chrissy smiled as though she was happy.

"I could also make some toast." Reno remembered that they had bought a new toaster and coffeemaker several years ago. He'd given the coffeemaker to Nicki for Christmas, and she'd given him the toaster. "We even have some homemade jelly from Mrs. Hargrove. I think its chokecherry. There's nothing like chokecherry jelly on toast."

"I've never had chokecherry jelly."

Reno had been counting on that. If he had any hope that Chrissy would be content on the ranch until they figured out what was happening with that lawyer, Reno would need to keep her entertained. Tasting a new kind of jelly wasn't much, but at the moment it was all he had.

"Did Mrs. Hargrove make the jelly?" Chrissy asked after she'd eaten a bit of the toast Reno had made. "From berries?"

"Why, is something the matter?" Reno didn't

think there could be any problem with jelly, but maybe he was wrong.

Chrissy shook her head. "It's just that I didn't know anybody made jelly anymore. I've only seen people buy it in the store."

Reno thought Chrissy looked a little worried. He stood up. "Oh, we have the store-bought kind, too—in the cupboard—if you'd rather have that. It's grape, I think. Let me get it for you."

Chrissy shook her head again. "No, thanks. I like Mrs. Hargrove's jelly better than any other jelly I've ever had."

Reno sat down. One thing was perfectly clear to him. He was never going to understand women. He would think that, since he'd had a sister all his life, he should know more about women. But then, Nicki had always said she didn't like all the things other women liked, like nail polish and shopping. Reno stopped. That was it.

"After breakfast we'll need to go shopping."

There, Reno told himself, that news should cheer her up. It seemed to work.

Chrissy beamed. "I can do that."

"It's on your job description." Reno nodded. He wasn't doing so badly, after all. A little shopping. Some different jelly. All of their problems would be solved.

Chapter Nine

Reno wondered what was wrong with him. He'd remembered his wallet, since they were going to do some shopping. He'd remembered the tire chains, since, even though the day was sunny so far, the mud was still thick on the road. But he had forgotten all about that dress.

Chrissy was wearing rubber boots on her feet because of the mud, and she had Justin cradled in her arms, but every man in the hardware store turned to stare at her in that midnight-blue dress when Reno opened the door and she walked through it.

Reno wondered how much of a sin it would be to take down each of his neighbors, some of whom were old enough to be his father. Of course, those two ranch hands from the Elkton spread were there, too, measuring out some nails for mending fence, and they were about Reno's age.

"Here, take this." Reno slipped out of his denim jacket and passed it to Chrissy.

He saw her start to protest, so he added, "It's not charity. It's just to keep you warm."

Chrissy looked at him and nodded. "Thank you, then."

Reno felt more pleased than he should that she had agreed to accept something from him. She was one of the most hardheaded women he knew when it came to her pride.

"Here, let me hold Justin while you put it on," Reno said next.

Chrissy handed him her baby, and Reno felt even more pleased. He hadn't had much holding time with the baby since they'd gotten to the ranch, and he missed it.

"Glad to see you made it to town to visit us," Elmer said from where he sat by the stove reading the Billings newspaper. He set the newspaper down on the floor and looked at Reno and Chrissy. "Didn't take you long."

Reno flushed. "We needed some supplies."

Elmer nodded. "I thought you might. Babies have a way of needing the craziest things. I remember when you were a baby. You had a special craving for applesauce. Your father used to have to make a special trip into Miles City just to get it for you.''

''That was Nicki.'' The older citizens of Dry Creek had a tendency to confuse Reno and his sister. Fortunately, they had both heard the stories for so many years, they could usually set the record straight.

''Ah, well then.'' Elmer picked up the newspaper and settled back to read it. ''I expect the little one won't be asking for that, then.''

There was a moment of silence.

''Reno's not the baby's father,'' Chrissy announced—a little too loudly, Reno thought. ''Even if Reno ate a tubful of applesauce, Justin won't be liking it, because they're not related.''

The store got even quieter.

''I wasn't meaning anything by my words,'' Elmer said softly from where he still sat. ''I was just remembering how babies are, and Reno and his sister came to mind—they were both cute as a button.''

''He's lucky he can remember that far back these days,'' Jacob said from the other chair.

''My mind's just as sharp as it ever was.'' Elmer stood up from his chair as though to prove it. ''Get out the checkerboard and I'll play anyone and prove it.''

The silence inside the store eased, and Reno heard the shuffle of feet as a couple of the men set the board up. Then the door opened.

"Ah, good, you're here," Reno said as Pastor Matthew entered the store.

Pastor Matthew worked as a relief clerk in the store in addition to preaching at the small church in Dry Creek. "You needed me? Store or church?"

"Store. Chrissy needs some new clothes. I was thinking maybe a pair of those farmer's overalls that you carry would work."

"Glory's coming right behind me. She's taken over the ordering of the stuff like the overalls, and she'll know right where to look for what you need."

Glory was the pastor's new wife. She was also an artist, and Reno had been hoping she would be around, so Chrissy could meet her. Not every small town in Montana had an artist.

Reno nodded in relief. "That would be good."

Chrissy liked the smell of Reno's jacket. Of course, it was probably because it smelled like the calves' feed supplements, and she was growing fond of the calves. They looked at her with big uncertain brown eyes, but she figured she could win them over after she held the milk bucket for them a time or two.

She was also fond of the smell of the tea she held in her hands. Elmer had offered her coffee, and Jacob had said she should drink tea instead of coffee because of Justin, and so Elmer had made her a cup of orange herbal tea. He'd poured the hot water into a real china cup, even though everyone else, even the two men slowly counting large nails into a brown paper bag beside the far shelf, was drinking from disposable cups.

"You don't need to give me a real cup," Chrissy said. Jacob had already given up his chair by the fire for her, and Reno was holding Justin while she drank her tea. She hadn't gotten this kind of courtesy when she was pregnant.

"I wouldn't want you to think we don't have manners," Jacob confessed as he stood by the store's window. "It's bad enough I don't know how to dance— I won't have it be said that I don't know ladies like their tea in a proper cup."

"Oh, I've been planning to tell you I'm interested in your ad for a dance teacher, if you still want to learn," Chrissy said before she took a sip of the fragrant tea. Jacob was right. She did like a cup for sipping. "Just tell me when."

"I don't know how to dance, either," said one of the men counting nails as he looked up from the bag he was filling. "I'm interested in dance lessons if you're teaching them."

Chrissy didn't recognize the man who spoke up. She knew he was working on the Elkton ranch, but she hadn't talked with those ranch hands when she was in Dry Creek last fall.

"Since when do you need to know how to dance?"

Reno said. He had been over by the counter, but he moved a little closer to Chrissy and frowned.

The ranch hand shrugged. "You never know when there's going to be a wedding. The last time I didn't know how to dance, and I felt I was missing out on the fun."

"No one's getting married in Dry Creek," Reno insisted.

Chrissy ignored Reno. She'd have to speak to him later about chasing away all her business. "I'm happy to teach you and Jacob at the same time. I'll even give you a group rate, since there's two of you. Does ten dollars an hour sound fair?"

"More than fair," Jacob said.

"I'd pay more than that to learn," the ranch hand agreed.

"I could use some brushing up, too," the second ranch hand said. "Count me in if you have space in your class. I don't think I've ever danced with a woman in a fancy dress like the one you're wearing."

"We're here to buy overalls for Chrissy," Reno said firmly. "That's what she'll be wearing if she teaches anyone to dance. Farmer overalls like Jacob over there wears."

Everyone in the hardware store turned to look at Jacob. Even Justin's eyes went in that direction.

Jacob was wearing well-worn denim overalls. The back piece snapped onto the front bib, at least on the right side of Jacob's front. He never kept the left side snapped into place because the metal hook had gotten bent in the washing machine and he hadn't taken the time to bend it back. "There's nothing wrong with my overalls."

"Actually, those overalls are kind of stylish." Chrissy glared at Reno. What was wrong with him today? "In fact, I've seen lots of women wear those overalls with halter tops, especially when it's hot outside."

"I hear the temperature is going to get into the seventies tomorrow," one of the two ranch hands said. "You might want to set a new fashion around here. Can't remember when I've last seen a pretty girl in a halter top."

Reno grunted. "She'll be wearing one of my work shirts with the overalls."

"Not when I'm dancing," Chrissy protested. She knew Reno was being protective of her, but he was going too far. "I'll teach dancing in a dress."

"Then it's the orange one," Reno said.

Chrissy looked up at Reno. His cap was pulled down, and it partially hid his face. But she didn't need to see his entire face to know that he was scowling at everyone. "You're going to scare Justin."

Reno looked down at the baby he held in his arms, and Chrissy saw his face visibly soften.

"He likes the orange dress, too, don't you?" Reno

murmured as he shifted Justin in his arms. "The two of us, we both think you should wear the orange one."

"The orange dress is fine," Chrissy said. "That is, if it's dry by then."

"It'll be dry," Reno promised.

Ten minutes later Chrissy was in the back room holding up a pair of striped farmer's overalls in front of her and looking in the long mirror Glory had set in a corner of the storeroom. Chrissy had taken off Reno's jacket, and the overalls covered up most of the blue Vegas dress as she held them up to the mirror.

"I'm sorry that the blue striped is the only color that we have in the small size," Glory said as she rummaged through a box on a nearby shelf. "But if I can find you a navy bandanna to twist around your neck, it looks kind of cute with a white T-shirt."

"Reno thinks I should wear his work shirts with the overalls," Chrissy said as she measured the length of the bibbed overalls against her legs. "So I don't think he'll give me a T-shirt."

"Oh, he won't, huh?" Glory looked up from the box of new bandannas and smiled. "Sounds like he wants to keep his competition down."

"Reno?" Chrissy stopped looking at the overalls. "He says we're almost cousins, so I don't think he's in the competition—if there is one."

"But you're not cousins."

"No, but he thinks so, and that's why he's being so protective. Garrett would be doing the same thing if he were here, and he *is* my cousin, so I guess that's really the way Reno feels."

All of a sudden shopping wasn't as much fun as it usually was for Chrissy.

"Besides, there's the church thing," Chrissy said before she realized she was talking to the wife of the Dry Creek church's pastor. "Oh, I'm sorry—I shouldn't have said—"

Glory waved away the apology with her hands. "Don't worry about it. So tell me, what's the church thing?"

"It's simple. He goes. I don't."

Chrissy stood on one foot so she could start to pull the overalls on under her blue dress.

Glory nodded. "I see. And you don't go because…?"

"I can take care of myself just fine. I don't need a group of church people trying to tell me what to do."

Glory laughed. "Well, I don't think I'd want that, either."

"But you're the pastor's wife." Chrissy looked at herself in the mirror. She had the overalls on up to her waist and the navy skirt of her dress bunched around her middle, making her look like some sort of exotic sausage that sparkled. "You're supposed to like all that church stuff."

"Oh, I do," Glory said. "But the church isn't there to tell people what to do. It's there because we all need God's help to live the life He wants us to live."

"Well, I don't need His help," Chrissy said as she prepared herself for an argument. "I can take care of myself and Justin."

Chrissy focused on looking at her chin in the mirror. She didn't want to see the look on Glory's face when she argued with her. Chrissy was already looking on Glory as a friend, and she didn't want to disappoint the other woman. But she had to be honest, too.

"I can remember the days when I used to think that about myself, too," Glory said as she held out a handful of bandannas to Chrissy. "Try one of the red ones, too."

"*You* thought that once? What happened?"

"A man tried to kill me," Glory answered calmly. "There's nothing like seeing a gun pointing at you to make you realize you need help from others and from God. Now—" Glory opened her hand so the bandannas were all visible "—you might want one of the green ones, too. And I think we have a small white T-shirt here someplace."

Reno hoped he had gotten his point across to Brad and Mark, the ranch hands from the Elkton place.

''You can dance, but no hands below the waist or above the waist. And I better see a good twelve inches of daylight between the two of you at all times.''

Reno had Justin cradled in his arms, and he was pacing back and forth in front of the two ranch hands as they finished counting out the nails they would need to mend the north fence later today.

''No one dances that way anymore,'' Brad protested.

Brad was the older of the ranch hands and too tall in Reno's opinion. Reno was a little under six feet himself, and he figured that was tall enough for anyone. But he knew some women measured a man by his height. He didn't know why. A tall man would never fit in Mrs. Hargrove's old car.

''You should probably dance in your socks, too,'' Reno said as he stopped his pacing a moment to look down at Justin. The baby was sound asleep. ''Leave your boots off. And maybe bend down a little, so you aren't so tall.''

''That's kind of hard to do when you're waltzing.''

Reno thought a minute. ''You're right. Maybe we should stick to line dancing.''

''Line dancing?'' Jacob protested. ''What happened to my waltz lessons?''

''Line dancing is more fun anyway,'' Reno said.

''Well, can I put my boots on if we're line dancing?'' Brad asked. ''I don't relish the thought of having my toes stomped on by Jacob or Mark.''

Reno nodded. This was going pretty well, and he was a fair man. ''If there's line dancing, you can keep your boots.''

''Good. My mother taught me it's polite to have my boots on the first time I kiss a girl.''

Reno forgot about being fair. ''There's no kissing. It's dance lessons, not kissing lessons.''

''Well, now, she might want to kiss me,'' Brad said as he stood up. ''Ever think about that? It's not like she's a shy young thing who's never been kissed before.''

There was a moment of shocked silence in the hardware store before Reno grabbed Brad's bandanna and pulled his face closer. ''Like I said, there's no kissing.''

''All right, all right,'' Brad said. ''No kissing.''

''I mean it.'' Reno released the cowboy's bandanna.

''No problem.'' Brad adjusted his bandanna. ''Don't know what your problem is, though. I don't see you dating her any.''

''She only got here yesterday.''

Brad smiled. ''So, have you asked her out?''

''She only got here yesterday,'' Reno repeated.

Brad's grin widened. ''I thought so. Coward?''

"He's not a coward," Jacob offered from where he sat by the fire. "He's her cousin."

"I'm not her cousin." Reno gritted his teeth. "I'm just a gentleman."

"Humph! If you were a gentleman, you wouldn't suggest she go dancing in farmer's overalls."

"I agreed to a dress." Reno decided it was time he took Chrissy over to the café for lunch. They might as well eat lunch in the café before they headed back to the ranch. That way, he could save his cooking skills for supper.

From what he could tell, he was going to have to do a lot of home cooking in the next few days if he wanted to avoid the men of Dry Creek. Why had he never noticed before that they all had only one thing on their minds and it was pretty women? He missed the days when they just talked about the mud outside and the price of cattle.

Chrissy had bought the white T-shirt on credit to wear with the overalls, and Glory was just giving the bandanna around her neck a finishing touch. Chrissy liked what she saw in the mirror. "This does look all right."

Glory nodded. "It's not quite as elegant as your blue dress, but it's cute."

"Thanks for giving me credit for the T-shirt. That way I won't have to borrow any shirts from Reno."

Glory nodded. "Don't want to do that, huh?"

"It just feels funny."

Glory smiled as she turned to hang up the other T-shirts that had come in the package of three. "Well, that's a good sign."

"Good sign of what?"

Glory turned around to look at Chrissy. "Let's just say that I'm guessing you wouldn't hesitate to borrow a shirt from Garrett."

"Of course not—Garrett's my cousin. More like a brother, really."

Glory nodded. "That's what I thought."

"What does that mean?" Chrissy asked. She was starting to have a funny feeling in her stomach. She couldn't be having those kinds of feelings for Reno, could she? Of course she knew he was an attractive man. But that was just because she had good vision. Any woman would know that.

"Don't look so alarmed," Glory said soothingly. "It probably doesn't mean anything."

"It's just that I don't want to be responsible for wearing one of his shirts in case I get it dirty when I feed the calves." Yes, that was it, Chrissy thought to herself. She was just a thoughtful borrower.

"I'm sure he wasn't going to give you one of his church shirts," Glory said. "He'd just give you one of his working shirts that he wears out in the barn."

"Oh." Chrissy frowned as she started to fold up

the blue dress. "I hadn't thought about that. You have to dress up to go to church."

Now, when in the conversation with Glory had she decided to go to church when she was in Dry Creek?

"The blue dress is fine."

"For church?" Even Chrissy knew she shouldn't wear a cocktail dress to church. "It glitters."

"Well, I have a dress you can borrow."

"I don't take charity." Chrissy put the blue dress over her arm and started to walk toward the door back into the hardware store.

Glory smiled. "I'll sell it to you."

"I don't have much money."

Glory stopped to push a box of nails back farther on a shelf. "Who's talking about money? I'd settle for an hour of rocking your baby some afternoon. The twins are getting a pretty good size these days, and they don't want to be rocked anymore. I kind of miss it."

Chrissy turned back to look at the other woman. "That doesn't sound like much to cover the cost of a dress."

Glory grinned. "If it's not enough, I'll cut the dress in half and sell you the skirt part."

Chrissy smiled, too. "I guess it would be all right to take the whole dress if it's an old one."

"We'll pick out the oldest dress in my closet,"

Glory said cheerfully as she opened the door back into the hardware store.

"Just so it's not orange." Chrissy stepped into the store.

"Sunday school is at ten. Reno will know the routine." Glory turned out the light in the storeroom and followed Chrissy into the store.

Chrissy heard a long, low wolf whistle when she stepped into the main room of the store. She automatically looked over to where Reno stood holding Justin, but his lips weren't puckered in a whistle. His face had a frown, though.

"You're looking good," one of the cowboys who stood next to Reno called out. "I'm going to enjoy those dance lessons."

Chrissy gave the man what she hoped was a businesslike smile. "Tonight at seven. In the bunkhouse at the Redfern Ranch." She looked over to Jacob. "If that time works for you, too?"

"I'll be there."

"So will I," Reno said as he scowled at the two cowboys.

"You're going to take dance lessons, too?" Chrissy asked as she looked over at Reno. With his natural grace, she had assumed he already knew how to dance.

"If I have to," Reno said grimly.

"I don't know if I can give four lessons at the same

time." Chrissy thought a minute. "I guess maybe two of you could pair up and dance together."

"What?"

Chrissy didn't know who looked more shocked, Reno or the two cowboys. Even Jacob looked a little whiter than before.

"I'll partner with Justin here," Reno said as he lifted up the baby. Justin gurgled in delight, as if he'd been lifted up high before and liked it.

"And leave me with Jacob?" one of the cowboys protested.

"I ain't dancing with you—you can dance with Brad there," Jacob said. "I'll get me a broom."

Chrissy left the men to their discussion and turned back to Glory. Only the two of them were standing beside the counter as Chrissy took a ten-dollar bill from her purse. "I'll have the rest of the money for the T-shirt for you next Friday."

Chrissy didn't like to be indebted to anyone.

Glory seemed to understand, and she spoke low so only Chrissy could hear. "That's fine. And stop by the house next to the church before you leave town. We'll pick out a dress."

Chrissy nodded. "Thanks."

Chrissy wondered if she had made the right decision. She hadn't even thought about deciding to go to church here in Dry Creek—she'd just been drawn to the people. She hoped they wouldn't expect too much if she came. She wasn't quite ready to jump into anything like religion.

Chrissy could still hear the men arguing on the other side of the store. "I can't sing, you know. I'd be no good in the choir."

Glory smiled. "I'm not in the choir, either."

"And I could never do any kind of public speaking. I don't really see that I'd be any good to the church."

"Don't worry about it."

"I don't even have any money to put in the collection plate. Well, until I get my check from my last job."

"You don't need to give anything, and I'd expect you to let us know if you need our help."

"I guess I could pour coffee sometime."

"Pour coffee where?" Reno said.

Chrissy had not seen him walk over to the counter.

"Nowhere," Chrissy said.

Reno eyed her suspiciously. "I hope you're not planning to be the one going around and pouring coffee at Jacob's big party. The coffeepot's too heavy, and the cowboys tend to be a little too friendly with the coffee pourers."

"Really? I never noticed," Glory said.

Reno nodded. "Remember that chef who catered the big dance Mrs. Buckwalter gave last spring? She poured coffee, and look what happened."

"She got married," Glory said. "The last I heard, she's expecting their first child."

"Yeah, well, I think she got a couple of proposals that night she poured coffee—and they weren't all from that rich man she married."

"Well, you don't need to worry about me getting married. I'm too busy taking care of Justin."

"Oh." Reno frowned as he looked down at the smiling baby in his arms. "He doesn't take that much work."

"Remember, I get to hold him for a while some afternoon," Glory said. "I could even drive out to the ranch and take care of him when you're working outside."

"Maybe when I feed the calves," Chrissy said. "Reno said he'd watch him, but I know he has other things to do."

"It's no trouble for me to watch him," Reno said

"That'll be perfect," Glory said. "What time this afternoon?"

Chrissy looked at Reno.

"Make it three o'clock," Reno said.

"See you then," Glory said as she reached out to give Chrissy a hug. "I'll look forward to it."

"Me, too," Chrissy said as she returned the hug. She felt as if she'd just made another friend. She'd never had so many friends in her life before.

"Here, don't forget your dress." Glory handed a

large paper bag to Chrissy as she started to walk toward the door.

"Thanks." Chrissy turned to take the bag.

Reno opened the door for her, and Chrissy stepped out onto the porch ahead of Reno and Justin.

"Thanks for taking care of Justin while I tried on the clothes," Chrissy said to Reno. "But I can hold him now."

The air was warmer than it had been earlier in the morning, and it looked as if the mud was finally going to start to dry.

"He's my buddy. I can carry him over to the café," Reno said as he stepped off the porch. "He's settled in."

Chrissy could see Justin was happy. The baby was gurgling up at Reno as if he were talking.

Chrissy frowned. Justin didn't have to be so friendly to the man.

Although Chrissy could not blame her son too much. There was something very charming about Reno. Maybe it was the way he scowled when he thought something was threatening her or Justin.

"So, what was that all about? With you and Glory?" Reno asked as they started walking across the street.

In the middle of the gravel road was a big puddle. But it didn't worry Chrissy. She had her farmer overalls tucked into the rubber boots she had borrowed from Reno before they came to town. She could ford a small stream if she needed to. It all gave her a sense of confidence in being able to meet whatever challenges lay ahead. "I'm góing to church."

"Here?" Reno looked dumbfounded.

Chrissy thought he didn't need to look so surprised. "Of course here. Sunday. There's a church, isn't there?"

"Of course." Reno started to smile. "So you're going to church?"

Chrissy nodded. "But I won't be singing any hymns or anything. I'll just be observing."

"Of course."

Reno's smile became even wider. Chrissy hoped he wasn't getting any ideas about what this all meant. "I think it'll be good for Justin."

Reno's smile turned into a grin. "Me, too."

Chrissy hoped she wasn't making a big mistake. She'd never gone to church before. Well, at least not where the people knew who she was. She was only getting a start in Dry Creek. Going to church might ruin everything, if the people treated her the way church people had treated her mother twenty years ago.

Chapter Ten

Reno decided he would ask Garth Elkton to take his place as an usher this next Sunday in church. Reno wanted to be sitting beside Chrissy in the pew throughout the entire service.

"Does Linda go to church?" Chrissy asked as she and Reno took the steps up to the porch outside the café.

Reno nodded. "She sings in the choir."

"So I won't be able to sit with her?"

"You can sit with me." Reno had never considered she would want to sit with someone else. He opened the door to the café. "I can help hold Justin."

"I don't think holding Justin is going to be a problem in this town. So far, everyone wants to hold him." Chrissy stepped into the café.

Reno's eyes had to adjust to the darkness inside. It

was already eleven o'clock, and the sun was starting to slide into its noon position. The clouds were gone for today at least, and the sun had already managed to dry up some of the mud.

There was no one in the front part of the café, but Reno could see through the open door into the kitchen area. Linda was leaning against the wall and talking on the phone. The air smelled of spaghetti sauce.

''I hope you like garlic,'' Reno said as he used one arm to pull a chair out so Chrissy could sit at one of the tables. He still held Justin in his other arm.

Chrissy lifted up her arms to Justin, and Reno could feel Justin squirm in recognition of her.

''I suppose I have to give him up.'' Reno bent to hand Justin to Chrissy.

The baby snuggled into his mother's arms, and Chrissy smiled down at him. It was all Reno could do to resist the temptation to stroke Chrissy's hair as she sat there. He could see why all the old masters used to paint pictures of the Madonna and Child. Chrissy was beautiful looking down at her baby. Her hair was a chestnut-brown that gradually grew lighter until it was blond at the tips. All her energy was focused on her baby.

Reno wondered what it would feel like to have all that love focused on him.

The faint scent of perfume floated up to Reno. ''Gardenia.''

Reno was pleased that Chrissy had worn perfume

for her drive to town with him. He hadn't expected it, but it was nice. A woman didn't put perfume on to impress a man she thought of as a cousin. Maybe he had a chance with her after all.

Chrissy looked up and then glanced down at the brown bag she'd set on the floor by her chair. "Oh, the gardenia was Jared's favorite. I used to wear it all the time for him. It's no wonder the scent is still on the blue dress."

"Oh."

"I think the bottle burned in the fire at my mother's house."

"If you like it, we could buy you another bottle."

"Thanks, but I don't wear perfume anymore."

"Oh."

Well, Reno decided, a man didn't get a clearer message than that. He wasn't one to talk about every emotion in the book, but sometimes a man needed to take a chance and speak up. "There's no reason to give up on men just because of someone like Jared. He wasn't half good enough for you, anyway."

Chrissy looked up at Reno with a wistful smile, and for one long heart-stopping minute Reno thought she was going to say something wonderful to him. Something like that she agreed with him and had no intention of giving up on men, especially him. Her rosy lips were moist, and her green-gray eyes were full of tenderness. She was almost going to speak.

Then the kitchen door slammed, and they both heard Linda at the same moment.

"Boy, do we have trouble." Linda didn't even hesitate to come walking out to the middle of the café where Chrissy sat and Reno still stood. "I'm glad you're both here."

"Is there something we can do?" Chrissy asked a little more politely than Reno figured he would have.

Reno did his best not to scowl. *This better be about something more important than burned spaghetti sauce or no Parmesan cheese to sprinkle over everything.*

"I just got a call from Jacob's nephew, David. He's going to be here in a few hours and wanted to get directions."

"I thought he already called," Reno said. Something wasn't right here, and he was glad Linda had the sense to be dramatic about it.

"No, he didn't call. That's the whole problem. He said he didn't call. He doesn't have a cell phone. And—" she paused "—he doesn't even know who Mrs. Robinson is—in the song."

"So that wasn't him who called the other day?" Chrissy asked.

Reno noticed that just the tiniest shadow of a frown was starting to form on Chrissy's face.

"That doesn't mean it was the guys who were around your mom's place the night of the fire," Reno said to reassure her.

"You don't think they started the fire there and are coming up here, do you?" Linda asked, aghast. "They might burn down the whole town."

Well, Linda might be a little too dramatic, Reno decided. "Nothing's going to burn around here. If the rain doesn't stop the fire, the mud will."

"I guess so." Linda nodded.

"Besides, millions of people have cell phones. There's no reason to assume the man who called is even coming here." Reno hoped his words made everyone relax.

"There might be millions of people with cell phones, but how many people drive a black car and play that Mrs. Robinson song? It's not even popular anymore." Chrissy wasn't easily convinced.

Reno noticed that Chrissy's knuckles were white as she clutched the blanket that was wrapped around Justin.

"We don't know the man who called was driving a black car. And that song—it could be playing on a radio anywhere."

"Maybe," Chrissy admitted.

Reno noticed her hands were relaxing. "Even if someone did come here, they wouldn't get close to you. The final road into Dry Creek is a private gravel road. I can put a roadblock up if you want. That way no one can come or go over the road."

Chrissy smiled a little sheepishly. "Well, maybe

after my dance students leave tonight. I'll feel safe as long as they're there.''

''And I'll watch the road during the day,'' Linda promised. ''A car has to drive past here if it's going to go out to the Redfern Ranch.''

''I forget how much different this is than Los Angeles. There's no way to block much of anything off down there.''

''Strange cars are noticeable here, too. We all know everyone's cars and pickups, so we know if a strange one is around,'' Linda added.

''And there's a long driveway into the ranch,'' Reno said. ''My dog, Hunter, always knows when someone's coming. There's no reason to worry.''

Just to be on the safe side, Reno planned to tell Sheriff Carl Wall about the problems with the lawyer and the suspicious fire in Los Angeles. But Chrissy didn't need to know about that conversation.

''I'll try not to worry,'' Chrissy said.

''Good.'' Reno nodded.

''I just need something to distract me,'' Chrissy added.

''You could have lunch,'' Linda suggested as she pulled her order pad out from the pocket of her waitress uniform. ''If that's what you came in for...''

''You have a uniform on,'' Chrissy said as she looked at Linda. ''I thought you hated uniforms and swore you'd never wear one.''

Linda leaned down. ''Jacob's nephew wanted formal service for the party he's giving for his uncle. If he's willing to pay for it, I decided I could wear a uniform. He promised there'd be a big tip, too." Linda looked at Chrissy. "I got another uniform in case you want one. I figured you can use a big tip as much as I can."

Chrissy shrugged. "Sure. I've worn worse uniforms when I've been working."

Reno nodded. "The ones in Vegas."

"I meant the orange one from Pete's Diner," Chrissy said. "The Vegas dresses are beautiful. They just need a dry cleaning to take the perfume scent out of them, and they'll be as good as new."

"If you want to help get the cake and the appetizers ready, you can come by tomorrow afternoon, too." Linda looked over at the baby in Chrissy's arms. "I suppose it's awfully expensive to raise a baby, isn't it?"

"It doesn't matter how much it costs," Chrissy said a little defiantly. "You can't put a price tag on a baby."

"I know," Linda whispered as though stricken. Her voice rose as she talked. "That's what I keep telling—people."

Linda's words ended on a hiccup of a sob, and she turned and ran back into the kitchen.

"Here. Hold Justin," Chrissy said as she stood up and handed her baby to Reno. "I've got to go find out what's wrong."

Reno couldn't help but notice that Justin didn't snuggle into his side the way he did when his mother held him. When he was on Reno's lap, the baby just stared up as if he expected to be entertained. "Yeah, well, I'd tell you what was going on if I knew a blessed thing to say about it all."

Justin gurgled up at him.

Reno smiled. "Well, I think it's going to be a while before lunch, so I guess I could tell you about the little pigs that went to market—but I need your toes."

Reno unwrapped a corner of Justin's blanket. "Now, the market that these little pigs went to wasn't like the grocery stores you see today. It was more like the hardware store. Remember when we were over at the hardware store? Well, that's the kind of place this market was that the pigs went to. It was a place where everyone kind of stayed around and talked."

It took Reno almost fifteen minutes to exhaust his store of nursery rhymes. He'd even thrown in the recipe for instant oatmeal so the baby would be able to cook for himself when the day came.

"No sense in thinking you won't need to cook," Reno said. "Women don't stay in the kitchen anymore, so if you want to eat, you'll have to know how to cook. Trust me. Fried potatoes get old after a while."

Now, when had Reno gotten tired of bachelor cooking? He never used to mind. For the first time since his sister had gotten married, Reno wondered if his father would have given them the same advice not to marry if he hadn't already been married and had the two of them. Eating every meal alone out at the ranch sounded less and less appealing as the days went by. Granted, Nicki and her husband were on the ranch property. But they were in their own house, and he couldn't eat every meal with them. No, it would just be him when Chrissy and Justin left. Him and his fried potatoes.

"Well," Reno said to Justin, "no sense in fretting about it. I can learn to cook something else. Starting with supper tonight." He looked down at Justin. "Maybe I can make something to impress your mother."

Reno looked around the café. There were tables and chairs and several water pitchers on the small serving table at the back. But he didn't see any menus.

"Of course, menus don't have the recipes with them anyway," Reno said. "Maybe it's better just to sit and think. Unless you want to tell me what your mother likes to eat?"

Reno looked down at Justin. The baby apparently didn't have any suggestions for supper.

"I also make a mean chili, but I didn't put out any beans to soak." Reno thought aloud. He wondered if Linda might have a frozen casserole that she would sell him. They had some funny Italian stuff they served sometimes. A little of that should impress Chrissy.

The door to the café kitchen opened, and this time both Chrissy and Linda came out. Even though they were smiling, Reno could tell they had both been crying. "Everything okay?"

"Everything is fine," Linda announced with her head held high. "I just don't think like a man."

Reno could tell he was in dangerous territory. "Good. I think."

"Men can be so stupid," Chrissy added cheerfully as she started walking back toward the table where Reno sat.

"I don't think Justin should be hearing this," Reno protested. He wasn't so keen on hearing it himself.

"Oh, not in the mental way," Chrissy said.

"What other way is there?" Reno didn't know if he should go on with this, but it seemed a little late to change the topic of conversation to the mud outdoors.

"There's such a thing as being stupid in the heart," Chrissy said as she stood beside Reno and held out her arms for Justin. "Come to Mama."

"Oh. What does that mean?" Reno lifted Justin up so Chrissy could hold him again.

"It means that not all men see how good it can be to have a baby," Linda explained as she came closer to the table, as well. "It doesn't matter if babies cost money, they are wonderful."

"Well, I certainly agree." Reno decided he finally knew how to make his way through this conversation. Women tended to worry about things like this, he supposed. Well, they shouldn't have worried. They should just have asked him. "Take Justin—in time, I could love him like he was my own son. I wouldn't care how much money it took to raise him."

There was stunned silence in the café.

"We weren't talking about Justin," Linda finally said softly.

"Oh." Reno thought a minute. "But he's the only baby around."

Linda looked at him as she pulled her order book from the pocket of her uniform. "And he'll probably *be* the only baby around since Jazz is so hardheaded he absolutely refuses to have a baby if we get married. He says they're too much money."

"Oh." Reno decided he'd already said too much.

"That's why Linda called the engagement off," Chrissy explained as she looked down at Justin. "She always assumed they'd have children."

"What man doesn't want to have children?" Linda continued, and then added with half a sob, "His parents had children. I always just assumed he would want them, too."

"Well, the two of you have been engaged a long time. I'm sure you can work it out. Maybe he didn't mean exactly *no* children," Reno said. "Maybe if you talked to him again—"

"No!" both women said in unison.

"He needs to be the one who comes to Linda," Chrissy explained. "That's the way it works."

Reno wondered how men and women ever got together. "But he might not know that's the way it works. Maybe he's waiting for her to come to him."

"Well, he'll wait until the day he dies, then," Linda said calmly as she reached into her pocket and brought out two small menus that she set on the table in front of Reno. "Now, can I take your order?"

"Did I smell spaghetti sauce?" Reno asked as he picked up a menu and looked at it. He was glad the conversation was returning to questions he knew how to answer.

"The spaghetti sauce burned."

"Oh. How about a cheeseburger?" Reno looked at the four remaining items on the menu.

"We're out of buns."

"I could have some pancakes."

Linda shrugged. "No milk to make the batter."

"The soup of the day?" Reno asked.

"It won't be ready until tomorrow. The beans are still soaking."

Reno finished looking at the menu. Chrissy was patting Justin on the back and she didn't look worried about what to eat. "That leaves the liver and onions."

"We don't really have that," Linda confessed. "Jazz just put it on the menu so it would look like we offered more things. We didn't think anyone would ever order it.''

Reno closed the menu. ''Do you have anything to eat?''

Linda thought. ''Not really. Jazz was the one who did the ordering and the cooking, and he's been gone for three days now.''

''I see.''

''We do have some imported mustard and a couple of frozen hamburger patties. I could fry you up a couple of those.''

''Sounds good,'' Reno said.

''Or we could wait for Mrs. Hargrove to get here,'' Chrissy offered. ''Linda called her before we came, and Mrs. Hargrove said she'd bring over some of the meat loaf she had left over from supper last night, along with some bread for sandwiches.''

''She's bringing some rice pudding, too. With raisins and cinnamon in it,'' Linda added. ''And then I'm going to put the closed sign up for a few hours this afternoon and go into Miles City and stock up on supplies. It isn't easy running the café if you're only one person.''

''Well, Jazz shouldn't have just left like that,'' Reno protested. What was Jazz thinking? It wasn't like him to be that irresponsible.

Linda blushed. ''I sort of told him to leave.''

''Ah.'' Reno thought a minute. ''So *you're* the one who told him to leave, but he's supposed to know that *he's* the one that needs to come back and apologize?''

"Of course." Linda looked at him in surprise. "I would think that's obvious."

"Do you happen to know where he's staying these days?'' Reno decided it wouldn't hurt to give Jazz a clue about what these rules were that men didn't know about.

"We put a down payment on the Jenkins place. So he's out there, I would imagine."

"You finally managed to get the down payment money!" Reno knew that they'd been working for over a year to pull that money together. "Congratulations!"

Someone knocked on the door of the café and Linda hurried over to open it.

"Mrs. Hargrove!" Linda held out her arms. "Here, let me take some of that so you can come inside."

"Oh, I don't have time to stay," Mrs. Hargrove said from outside the door.

"The baby's here."

"Oh." Mrs. Hargrove stepped inside the café and looked around. "Chrissy's baby?"

Mrs. Hargrove had a large, foil-wrapped packet in one hand and a loaf of bread in a plastic bag in the other hand. She set both of them on a table beside the door and stood there. She wore a blue gingham dress with her black sweater over it and a four-cornered scarf on her head.

Chrissy's heart started beating fast. She knew Reno had said Mrs. Hargrove wanted her here, but he could be wrong. He might have just been polite when he said that. "Hello, Mrs. Hargrove."

Mrs. Hargrove walked closer and whispered, "He's not sleeping, is he?"

Chrissy looked down at Justin. His eyes had closed. "Maybe a little bit. He sleeps a lot."

"Babies do that." Mrs. Hargrove nodded as she walked closer still. "I'd forgotten how tiny they are. How old is he now?"

Chrissy blushed. "Eight weeks."

Justin stirred in his sleep and yawned.

"Don't you think he's a little small for his age?" Reno asked with a frown. "I think we should take him to Dr. Norris and have him weighed."

"He's just about perfect," Mrs. Hargrove said as she looked down at Justin. "Besides, his mother is small boned. Maybe he takes after her."

Chrissy couldn't stand it. "He doesn't have a father to take after. Well, I mean, of course he has a father. Everyone has a father. It's just—" Chrissy took a deep breath. "He doesn't have a father in the legal sense."

Mrs. Hargrove smiled as though that fact didn't bother her at all. "What's done is done. I'm just hoping you'll let us make up for that and do some of what a father would."

"Huh?" Chrissy figured she hadn't heard right.

Mrs. Hargrove said, "We'd love to help take care of your baby."

"You don't care if I'm not married?"

"Well, of course I'd love to see you get married." Mrs. Hargrove looked at Reno. "To some fine young man."

Chrissy swallowed. She couldn't even look at Reno. "Am I on some kind of list at the church? Is that why you're being nice to me?"

Mrs. Hargrove laughed. "The only list we have is a prayer list. Besides, no one needs a reason to be nice to you."

Chrissy wasn't so sure about that, but she didn't think she'd figure out anything by asking more questions. Maybe when she went to the church she would find out what the deal was. She'd die of mortification if a prayer that she would get married was written out somewhere.

"Now, I hear you need some lunch," Mrs. Hargrove said as she stepped back to the packages she'd left on the table. "Let me get the meat loaf to the back while it's still warm. It makes a wonderful sandwich with grilled toast, and I think Linda already has the toast going."

"I've never seen anyone bring food to a restaurant before." Chrissy looked over at Reno. He wasn't frowning, so that must mean he hadn't seen the look Mrs. Hargrove had given him when she mentioned that Chrissy should be married.

"There are some good things about being in a small town," Reno said. "I mean, meat loaf might not be gourmet, but it's filling."

Chrissy wondered if it was the smell of that meat loaf that had kept Reno distracted. "I love meat loaf."

"Good, because we're having it for supper tonight, too."

"Sounds fine."

Justin moved again and woke up, so Chrissy looked down at him. "He doesn't look like Jared much at all."

"Good." Reno nodded.

"Well, maybe around the eyes he does a little."

"The color of his eyes will change as he grows," Reno said.

"Have you been reading baby books?" Chrissy asked in surprise. Reno never ceased to amaze her.

Reno shook his head. "I just know from watching kittens and other animals."

Chrissy nodded. "And the calves."

"Oh, their eyes mostly are always brown."

"I bet they're getting hungry again," Chrissy said.

Chrissy had watched Reno feed the calves this morning, but this afternoon he had promised to let her hold the bucket. She was looking forward to it.

Chapter Eleven

Chrissy was glad she had her overalls and boots to wear. She was in one of the corrals on the Redfern Ranch, and all twelve calves wanted to butt against her legs. She didn't know what they would have thought if she'd been wearing her Vegas blue dress. They'd probably be trying to eat the sequins right now. A couple of the bigger calves pushed their way closer to her, trying to get their heads near the bucket she held even though she had told them clearly that it wasn't their turn and that other calves were eating at the moment.

"They just don't listen," Chrissy said as she looked over at Reno. He'd stepped a few feet closer to the fence, saying he wanted her to see what it was like to be alone with the calves.

The afternoon had turned sunny, and Chrissy

thought that might be why the calves were so playful. The clouds had gone away as she and Reno drove back from Dry Creek, and the sun was warm enough that neither one of them needed a jacket.

Chrissy was glad that Glory had driven out to sit with Justin today, because she wanted Reno's full attention to be on her while she fed the calves for the first time. When a calf nursed at the rubber bucket spigots, he tended to push the bucket around with his head. It was all Chrissy could do to keep control of the bucket. Calves, she learned, didn't have any sense of etiquette.

When one of the calves finished all the milk in the bucket, Chrissy would swing around and grab a full bucket from the shelf that ran along the edge of the barn. If she wasn't fast enough, the calves would start to nudge her.

"You'll probably need to push that big one away, the one with the white spot on his forehead," Reno said. "He always wants to eat. I call him Piggy."

Chrissy giggled. Reno had a name for each of the calves. "Don't you think he'll get confused about what kind of an animal he is?"

"Him? He's not very philosophical. He doesn't care what he is as long as he's well fed. He'd probably rather be a pig."

"Ahh, he's not a bad calf," Chrissy said as she reached out to pat Piggy. The calf turned his head, however, and she ended up patting his wet tongue.

The calf had been hoping she had something to eat in her hand. "Ugh, Piggy."

Chrissy wiped off her hand.

"See?" Reno had moved a step closer, but not close enough that the calves gave their attention to him. As long as Chrissy held the feeding bucket, she was their favorite.

"Be careful of Graceful there," Reno added.

Chrissy looked down at the small calf with the big brown eyes that was standing close to her right side. Graceful, Reno had told her, liked to come in close and, because she was small, could slip in around the other calves. Of course, to get that close, she had a tendency to step all over the toes of whoever was holding the feeding bucket.

"How do you think of all these names?" Chrissy asked.

Reno shrugged. "The same way anyone thinks of a name. How did you come up with the name Justin?"

"I named him after my father," Chrissy said as she gently shoved Graceful away from the bucket.

"Really? I didn't think you knew who your father was." Reno came closer and pushed Piggy to the outskirts of the calf herd.

"I don't," Chrissy admitted as she looked up at Reno and gave a small smile. "I just thought I knew the name for a while. I went through a period where I begged my mother to tell me my father's name. A couple of times I thought she started to say his name, but all that came out was 'Just—'. Of course, I decided his name was Justin.''

''Well, wasn't it?''

Chrissy shook her head. ''Turns out my mother was going to say 'Just stop asking me' or 'Just forget about it' or something. But I'd already started calling my father Justin in my mind, so I decided to continue. After all, he had to have a name.''

Chrissy kept her eyes focused on the calves while she answered Reno's question. She wanted him to know about her father and she hoped he would understand, but she didn't want to look him in the eye in case he didn't quite see it her way.

''Of course he needed to have a name,'' Reno said indignantly. ''You needed something to call him, and Daddy sure wasn't it.''

Chrissy winced. How did he know that had been a sore place in her heart?

''One of the hardest things I ever did was call Lillian 'Mother' again after she came back last fall,'' Reno continued. ''It had been all I could do to call her Lillian for all those years when she was gone. I didn't want to name her at all.''

Chrissy nodded. So that was how he knew. ''Your mother is sorry about hurting you and Nicki when she left—at least, that's what she's said. She used to talk about her children when I knew her in Vegas.''

Reno nodded. "I know she's sorry. It's still hard for me to call her Mother."

"Yeah," Chrissy murmured. "I wonder if parents ever think about how it is for kids."

Piggy pushed to be closer to the bucket at the same instant that it all flashed in Chrissy's mind. "What's Justin going to call his father?"

"He won't be worrying about that for a while." Reno stepped in closer still and put his hand on the feeding bucket next to where Chrissy held it. "He can't even talk yet. You've got plenty of time to figure it out."

"Maybe I should let his grandmother raise him," Chrissy said. "At least then he'd get to hear all about his father. It's important for a boy to know who his father is. Really, maybe even more important than knowing who his mother is."

"I don't know about that," Reno said slowly. "Mothers are pretty important."

Chrissy let Reno take full control of the bucket so she could think. "I thought telling my mother about Jared was hard. Wait until I have to tell Justin about him."

"Kids are pretty understanding."

"Were you?"

Reno didn't know how to comfort Chrissy. "No, I guess I wasn't very understanding. But I grew up all right. Every kid has to make his peace with something."

Chrissy reached up and gathered her hair into a twist at the back of her head. "But usually they only need to make their peace about the fact that the Easter bunny isn't real and the tooth fairy isn't going to leave a dime under their pillow every time something painful happens."

"So Justin will turn out stronger than most. He'll be loved. That makes a big difference."

"I don't know if I can be enough for him."

Chrissy looked more scared than Reno had ever seen her, even on the night when they were racing back to the fire at her mother's house. Her shoulders were hunched, and she didn't even notice that Graceful was stepping on her toes.

"You won't be alone with Justin," Reno said. "You don't have to be everything to him. You've got people who care."

Chrissy had never had people, outside of her mother, whom she could count on. "I thought Mrs. Hargrove was just being polite when she said she'd help."

"She wasn't," Reno said. "And I'll be there and Garrett will be there."

"And I can really handle most things myself," Chrissy added. "All I'll need is a little help."

"And we can give you more than that."

Reno saw the old Chrissy emerge as she talked. She was confident and smiling again. "As long as

I'm in Dry Creek, we'll be fine, then. I'll just have to stay.''

Reno was speechless. Chrissy had just said she was going to live in Dry Creek. He had never wanted to hear any words as much as he wanted to hear those. But it wasn't right. ''You don't need to stay because you're scared of what will happen if you leave. We'd all still be there for Justin no matter where you live.''

''Don't worry. I won't expect this job to last forever. I know these calves will be able to eat grass pretty soon— or hay, or whatever it is you're feeding the others.''

''It's not about this job,'' Reno protested. ''I want you to stay in Dry Creek. I'm just worried you'll—'' Reno stopped himself. He hadn't meant to say all of this out loud, but maybe he needed to. ''It's just that Dry Creek isn't like Las Vegas.''

Chrissy was frowning at him. ''Well, of course it's not.''

''We don't have any shops where you can buy those fancy dresses. We don't have any beauty salons. We don't have any gourmet restaurants. And you think you can live without them now, but you're wrong. All women like those kinds of things.''

Chrissy's frown turned to a smile. ''You're brilliant. That's absolutely right.''

''What?'' Reno hadn't thought she would agree so easily. And she didn't need to look so happy about it. She could at least have pretended to think about staying in Dry Creek, as she had said she was going to do. "Shouldn't you at least think about Justin a little more? We have lots of fishing around here. And horses. Little boys love to ride horses."

"Justin can't even walk yet. He's too young to ride horses." Chrissy finished feeding the last calf and swung the bucket up on the shelf. "I need to go inside and talk to Glory. I'll come clean the buckets a little later, before the guys come for a dance lesson."

Reno figured he might as well clean the buckets. He hoped Nicki and Garrett came back from their trip soon. He didn't understand women at all, and now that Nicki had found love, maybe she could help him out.

Chrissy lined her lips with the darkest red lipstick that she had. Jared had called this her "kissing lipstick," although he had never kissed her when she had it on because he said it made his lips look red, as well. Still, she looked very dressed up when she wore it with blush and eye shadow and her diamond-chip earrings.

She already had the blue dress on, so she'd just need to sweep her hair up into a French braid to have exactly the look she wanted. She had looked at the orange dress as it hung on the hanger and couldn't bring herself to wear it. Tonight, she told herself, was important. She wanted each of her dance students to go back and report to everyone else in town that she looked beautiful.

A report like that would make it much easier to put her plan into action. When Reno was describing Dry Creek to her earlier this afternoon, she'd realized he was absolutely right. There was no beauty salon for women in Dry Creek. And the women wouldn't want just a beauty salon. They would want a place to visit and buy soaps and perfume. The men had the hardware store. The women needed a place, too.

Chrissy wasn't totally naive. By now she had figured out that half, or maybe all the jobs on that job board in the café were fake. Oh, someone was willing to pay her to do what the ad asked. It was just that the ad wouldn't be there at all if she didn't need the work.

It was a kind gesture from many people in Dry Creek. But she couldn't build her future on feeding Reno's calves or doing Elmer's mending. She needed to have a real job.

Or, better yet, she needed to have a business—and a beauty shop could be it. She had wanted to go to beauty school after she graduated from high school, but Jared had wanted to move to Las Vegas, and she'd thought it wouldn't hurt to work as a waitress for a year or so before they settled down.

But now, when she looked at her life, she knew she needed to have a plan.

Chrissy snapped a hair clip into place and

smoothed a few strands of hair off her neck. The first step to her plan would be to impress her dance partners. To do that, she should be ready when they came to the door.

She looked out the window. The night was dark on the Redfern Ranch, but she saw the lights of a pickup as it drove down the long road into the main part of the ranch. That would be her students. The two cowboys from the Elkton Ranch had said they'd stop in Dry Creek and pick up Jacob on their way.

Well, she was ready for them.

She had Reno's coffeemaker plugged in to the outlet by the table in her makeshift kitchen. She also had a plate of cookies Mrs. Hargrove had given her as a welcome gift before she and Reno left Dry Creek earlier today. Justin was dozing in the crib by her bed. She hoped to keep the music down low enough that he would sleep through the lessons.

Chrissy went over to the CD player that Linda had lent her for the lessons. Linda said the player was only taking up room on the counter in the back of the café and that Chrissy was welcome to use it until Saturday night. The café advertised music with dinner on Saturday night.

"It used to be live music," Linda had said. "But since Jazz isn't here to sing and play his guitar, I hope people will be happy with some CDs. I have a pretty good selection of music."

Linda had lent Chrissy some waltz music, and

Chrissy was planning to give her a few dollars after she collected the fees from her students tonight.

Chrissy sighed. She'd been so determined to be independent and not take charity from anyone, but it seemed as if she was getting help from everybody. She really should get a notebook and write it all down, so she could pay it back when she was able.

"Anyone home?" Reno's voice called out softly as he knocked on the door.

Chrissy went over to the door and opened it.

"Oh." Chrissy had never seen Reno in a suit. He was freshly shaven and smelled of something herbal. The suit was black, and his shirt was snow-white and open at the collar. She could see his throat as he swallowed.

"Am I early?"

"Ah, no." Chrissy knew she was staring. But she had just never expected Reno to look like this. She knew he was handsome, of course. But she'd always thought his good looks were of the kind that were at their best in blue jeans and flannel shirts. She'd never thought of what he would look like in formal clothing. Now she knew.

"Is something wrong?" Reno asked.

Chrissy blushed. "I just never thought you'd look like this in a suit."

"I can change it. It's just what I wear dancing."

"You look very nice. I was just surprised, that's all."

"Oh." Reno smiled. "Well, you look very nice, too."

"Thank you." Chrissy realized they were still standing on the porch. She stepped to the side. "Oh, I'm sorry, come in. The others will be here in a minute."

Chrissy could hear the sounds of the pickup as it made the final turn into the road that led to the main ranch house. It would have to make another turn to come down to the bunkhouse.

"I was hoping if I got here early, there'd be time for a dance before the others started," Reno said.

"Oh, I couldn't possibly. I mean, it's just the lessons."

Chrissy wasn't sure she'd feel right about dancing with Reno all alone in the bunkhouse. It made her breath come up short just thinking about it.

Reno shrugged. "It's just that I hate to make a fool of myself in front of the other guys."

"Oh, I see." Chrissy told herself she needed to forget about Reno's startling good looks. Tonight he was just a student who needed a little extra practice. She went over to push the button on the CD player. "I can see how you wouldn't want to do that."

The sounds of an instrumental waltz played softly in the kitchen.

"I'm trying to keep the music down so that Justin can sleep," Chrissy said as she stood in position to dance with her first student.

"We don't need much in the way of music," Reno said as he reached behind his back and turned off the switch to the main overhead light in the bunkhouse. Only a lamp in the far corner by the bed gave off light as he put his hand on Chrissy's waist and drew her to him so they could waltz.

"We should leave the big light on."

"Hush, we don't want to wake Justin. Leaving the light off will help him sleep."

Chrissy supposed he was right.

Reno's life was complete. He hadn't known it would feel so good to hold Chrissy in his arms, even if she was counting in his ear and trying to lead. She had pulled her hair back and put it up in some kind of an elegant braid. If it weren't for the few rebellious strands of hair that escaped the braid, she would look so perfect he'd think she wasn't real.

It was those strands of hair that were his undoing. He couldn't help but lift them off her neck. The skin of her neck was like warm silk. Her hair was even softer. And there, right at the base of her throat, he could see her pulse fluttering like a butterfly.

"I didn't have any pins," Chrissy said as she stopped dancing and looked up at him.

It took Reno a second to know what she was talking about. "You don't need pins for your hair. It's beautiful like this."

Once Reno had smoothed back her hair, he noticed the small wisps around her ear and he tucked those back, as well. When his hand rested against the side of her neck, he could feel her pulse.

Chrissy was looking up at him.

Reno knew he shouldn't kiss her. But his life to this day seemed long, and all the days following this moment seemed short. Sometimes a man just needed time to be frozen for a second so he could think.

Reno forgot his hand was still resting along the side of Chrissy's throat until he felt her pulse with his fingertips. The beat of her pulse was increasing. And she was looking at him with eyes that waited.

Reno bent his head slowly. He wanted her to have time to signal him that she wasn't ready for a kiss. He would have stopped at the last minute if it killed him rather than force her into a kiss.

But no signal came, and his lips met hers. Suddenly the days that had seemed so short spreading before him now began to seem long, because nothing in them would match this moment of time.

A small circle of soft light came in the window of the bunkhouse.

Chrissy was the first to pull away. "That's the lights from the pickup. The others are here."

Reno nodded. He couldn't speak yet.

Chrissy swallowed. "I don't usually kiss men on the first date—" She stopped. "Not that this is a date or anything."

"It could be," Reno said. "We could tell the others

the lessons are off. I could take you to Miles City, and we could see a movie or something.''

For the first time in his life Reno thought that the home he'd surrounded himself with was too small. He needed to think bigger. For a moment he wished he lived in a big city. If he did, there would be someplace he could take a woman like Chrissy on a date that would show her how important she was to him. Everything around here seemed too ordinary. ''We could even drive down to Las Vegas and see one of the entertainers there. Something with fireworks.''

''Las Vegas.'' Chrissy looked startled. ''We just came through there.''

''I know. But just because we're in Dry Creek doesn't mean we can't drive someplace else for some excitement.''

Chrissy frowned and touched his lips with her fingers. ''I didn't mean to get lipstick all over. Let me get something to wipe off the lipstick.''

''Forget my lips for a second.'' Reno heard the sounds of heavy footsteps on the steps that led up to the porch of the bunkhouse. He didn't have much time. She wasn't even really listening to him. ''I've even thought it would be fun to go to Paris some day.''

''Paris! You've never mentioned Paris.''

Now he had done it, Reno thought. Chrissy was looking at him with more suspicion than longing in her eyes. She must think he wasn't serious.

Chrissy had found a tissue somewhere and wiped his lips with it.

"A man doesn't need to stay on the same piece of land he was born on," Reno said when he could. "Sometimes he needs to reach for more."

It sounded as if an army was knocking on the bunk-house door.

"I better let them in," Chrissy said as she reached for the door handle.

Brad was the first one through the door, and his eyes went straight for Reno. "What's going on here?"

"I was just giving Reno a little extra help with his dancing," Chrissy said as the three men all stepped into the room. "Hi, Jacob. Brad. And Mark, isn't it?"

Brad grunted and grinned at Reno. "Need extra help, do you?"

Reno nodded. It certainly looked to him as if he could use some extra help. Not that he trusted Brad to be able to give it to him.

No, Reno decided, what he needed was a little divine intervention. He felt a little odd asking God to give him enough money to take a girl someplace so he could impress her. Reno had grown up learning to be content with what he had and pretending some things, like having a mother, didn't matter. After all, he had a sister and a father.

Reno was good at knowing the limits to how much he could expect. He'd always thought that was what

God wanted. No, it wasn't likely He would okay a trip to Europe. God would probably tell him that a good marriage proposal didn't require Paris anyway.

Oh—Reno stopped himself. When had he decided to ask Chrissy to marry him? Surely that wasn't a good idea. The two of them? He stamped down the hope that rose in his throat. That was clearly outside the limits. Wasn't it?

Chapter Twelve

Reno sat on the rocker on the bunkhouse porch and cradled Justin in his arms. The baby had woken up after about two rounds of waltzing, and Reno was relieved to be able to take him outside on the porch and rock him. Of course, Reno positioned the rocker so that he could see through the window and watch Chrissy conduct her lessons.

"She's good," Reno admitted to Justin as they sat in the darkness.

Chrissy was taking her teaching seriously. Even Brad was frowning and trying to match his steps to some tape she'd put on the floor.

The golden light from inside the bunkhouse filtered out into the darkness of the porch and Reno could hear the faint sound of music with a strong beat. The Montana night was dark and moonless. Reno's dog,

Hunter, had curled up at the foot of the rocker and was lying there just as though he'd forgotten he was part wolf and shouldn't be so happy to be domesticated.

"Must be more clouds up there," Reno said to Justin by way of information. He'd already introduced him to Hunter and explained about dogs. "You remember clouds? Those big white things in the sky that look like pillows."

It was amazing all the things a baby had to learn.

Until he'd had Justin around, Reno had never thought about what he would be missing if he didn't have a child. He liked to hold Justin and think of all the things that he could share with the boy as Justin grew older. There could be fishing trips and baseball games.

"And some cooking lessons, too," Reno reminded him. "Some of these jobs are equal opportunity now. We won't just leave it all to your little sister. And the laundry, too."

Reno knew he was dreaming. But what could it hurt to dream for a night? The desire to marry Chrissy and have a family with her had taken hold in him, and he deserved at least one night of wondering what it would be like before he actually said anything to her and heard her answer.

He knew he didn't have a chance. And it wasn't just that he really couldn't afford to take her to Paris. After all, Chrissy seemed to be enjoying her time in

Dry Creek, but he still didn't think she would stay for long. She was visiting.

Of course, she'd surprised him already when she'd made her decision to go to church this next Sunday. She'd talked about where to sit and what to wear enough so he knew that she fully intended to go, and not as a visitor. No, she was trying to find where she fit with the church and with God. He hoped that meant she intended to give God a fair chance in her life.

But even if she made her peace with God, it didn't mean she would want to stay in Dry Creek.

Reno knew the reason Chrissy was in Dry Creek was that she was scared. But she had told that fire captain her suspicions about Mrs. Bard's attorney and had given him Jared's phone number in Las Vegas. Reno expected that someone had at least questioned the attorney by now. The authorities might even have talked to Jared.

The custody issues with Justin would calm down soon. When the fire authorities started to ask the attorney questions, Reno knew the man would stop his harassment and Chrissy would feel free to go anywhere. Reno would be happy when that day came except for one thing—if Chrissy was free to live anywhere, she wouldn't choose to stay in Dry Creek.

Reno wondered where Chrissy *would* choose to live. He looked down at the baby looking up at him.

"My guess would be Los Angeles, wouldn't you say, sport?"

Reno had decided that Justin was a long name for a baby and he had experimented with nicknames. He'd tried out "Jus," but that sounded like an old man. He'd moved on to "sport." It wasn't quite right, but it was closer.

Hunter moved slightly at his feet, and Reno looked down. The dog had tensed up as though he heard something.

Reno turned from the window and looked out into the dark night away from the bunkhouse. He could see the tall outlines of the trees around the main house and the angles of the barn. He'd left the yard light on, so he could see the circle of packed dirt between the bunkhouse and the main house that everyone used for parking. There were no strange cars there. Just the two pickups—his and Brad's.

Everything looked normal, but Reno trusted Hunter's instincts, so he stood up and moved out of the light from the window so he could see better. He let his eyes adjust and looked over at the barn. There was always a little noise on the ranch. A cow might be mooing or a chicken scratching at the ground.

Reno looked around the corner of the bunkhouse so he could see the long road that led into the ranch. He didn't see any lights of approaching vehicles. He had never fully relaxed since Linda had said that the man who had called the café asking for directions to

Dry Creek wasn't Jacob's nephew. But unless someone was crawling on his belly through the pasture directly in front of the bunkhouse, no one was around who shouldn't be here.

"Is it maybe just a rabbit?" Reno asked the dog standing at his feet. Hunter didn't always care whether the intruder was a six-foot human or a six-inch rabbit. Either way, he went on alert.

"Or do you feel something coming?" Reno frowned into the darkness. Hunter seemed to sense when a car was coming. Reno had often wondered if the dog felt vibrations from the distant vehicles before they even turned onto the drive that led up to the Redfern Ranch.

Whatever it was that Hunter had heard, the dog must have decided it was all right, because he went back and lay down beside the rocker again.

"Well, we should probably go inside before too long anyway," Reno muttered as much to himself as to Justin. "You need your sleep, and those lessons should be about over."

Reno would feel better if the ranch hands left and he could go put up the roadblock he'd nailed together late this afternoon. The roadblock was a bunch of wooden sawhorses and some metal sheeting he'd had in the barn.

Even though someone could get past the roadblock, he would make enough noise to wake Reno as well as Hunter. Especially since Reno intended to sleep in the barn on the cot he kept for calving season. That way, he could hear anything coming down the road better than if he was in his cozy upstairs bedroom in the main house.

Chrissy knew her breath was coming in soft, quiet gasps. "The boys," as she'd referred to them all night, had decided to teach her how to do a down-home cowboy line dance as a thank-you for teaching them how to waltz. They didn't have a CD with the right music, so the three of them took turns calling out a beat.

The furniture in the bunkhouse was already pushed to the wall or moved out to the porch, but it still hadn't seemed as if there was enough room for all the swirling and stomping.

Chrissy had had to hold up the long skirt of her blue dress when it came to some of the stomping sets, and she realized she must have looked a sight with all her sequins sparkling and her hair falling out of the French braid on her head. She would have done better in a cotton square-dance outfit, but she was glad she'd decided not to wear the orange dress.

"Now, that's a man's dance," Jacob said in satisfaction. He was breathing hard, too, and he had a big smile on his face. "I think it must come from Ireland or somewhere."

The main light in the room gave off a bright light. Reno had turned it on when the three men arrived.

Since Justin had already woken up with all the pounding at the door earlier, Chrissy had decided to leave the light on.

Not that it mattered now anyway, since Justin was out on the porch with Reno. Of course, she doubted Justin was sleeping, even though there were no bright lights out there to disturb him. Justin never seemed sleepy when he was with Reno. He always seemed to want to stay awake and see what was happening.

"It's not a man's dance," Brad protested as he leaned against a wall so he could put his boots back on. Brad was wearing a white shirt with a black cowboy tie and what he had said earlier were black snakeskin boots. "If a man's going to go to the trouble of getting all dressed up for dancing, he likes to hold a woman when he's dancing, and in that one you only twirl her around."

"Oh, let me get you a chair." Chrissy looked around. Where were her manners? A man shouldn't have to stand to put on his boots. Had they put all the chairs out on the porch? She'd had two chairs at the table earlier.

"I'm fine." Brad waved the offer away. "I don't want to bother Reno. At least, not now that I'm getting my boots back on."

Brad smiled when he said that, and the other two men nodded and chuckled.

"Why would he care if you have your boots on or

not?'' Chrissy wondered if she was missing some cowboy humor.

''I told him a gentleman only kisses a lady when he has his boots on,'' Brad said with a long, lazy drawl to his words and a new something in his smile.

Chrissy blinked.

''Not that a gentleman even brings the subject up,'' Jacob said with a frown at Brad before turning to Chrissy. ''I wouldn't want you worrying about him. He's just got a peculiar way of joking. Don't pay him any attention.'' He turned back to Brad. ''For some fool reason he thinks all woman want to kiss that ugly mug of his.''

''Who are you calling ugly?'' Brad demanded to know with more energy than he'd put into the rest of the conversation.

Chrissy was relieved to see that, in truth, Brad would rather argue with Jacob than kiss her. She decided there must be something about this dark Montana night that made men want to take up kissing. She shouldn't think it meant much.

As she recalled, Linda had told her stories last fall about the old days at the Redfern Ranch when the cowboys had held a kissing auction or two. It must be something about this ranch area.

Chrissy looked up to see the door to the bunkhouse opening.

''Someone's coming,'' Reno announced as he stepped into the bunkhouse. He decided he was grateful the other three men hadn't left yet. If there was going to be trouble, all three men would be good to have around. "I don't know who it is, but Hunter noticed someone was coming first and I can see the lights coming down the road."

"Who'd be coming here?" Jacob asked. "We're almost finished with the dance lessons."

"I'm sure they're not coming to dance," Reno said as he felt Justin squirm. Without thinking much about it, Reno shifted Justin in his arms so the baby could see better.

Reno was glad he'd left the yard light on. At least he'd be able to see what kind of vehicle was coming down the driveway.

"Well, maybe it's just a neighbor coming by to visit," Chrissy said.

"Maybe," Reno said. He didn't tell Chrissy that neighbors around here didn't drop by to visit someone this close to midnight. Everyone was in bed at this hour. Of course, if there was an emergency, that would be a different matter. But then they'd usually call first.

"I don't suppose anyone heard the phone from the house ringing earlier?"

Jacob shook his head. "We wouldn't have heard a phone even if it was down here in the bunkhouse."

Reno nodded. Now that it occurred to him, he hadn't checked the answering machine in the house since breakfast. He and Chrissy had been in town, and he'd been busy after that. "Maybe someone called earlier to say they'd be over this evening."

"Your neighbor Lester did say he was feeling lonely these days. Maybe he's coming over to talk," Chrissy said.

"Lester?" Jacob said in astonishment as he walked over to the window and looked out. "He doesn't even say much in the middle of the day. What would he need to say at midnight?"

"Whoever it is, you can't see them out that window yet." Reno heard his sister's horse, Misty, neigh from the corral by the barn. Even the chickens sounded as though they were flapping around in their coop. Whoever was coming up the drive wasn't bothering to be quiet about it.

"That's Big Blue," Chrissy said. "I'd recognize those gear changes anywhere."

"Garrett's truck? He wouldn't be grinding his gears like that." Reno's new brother-in-law was a legend in trucking circles, and he would no more grind the gears on his big rig than a cowboy would shoot his favorite horse.

"I don't think it's Garrett driving," Chrissy said as she walked toward the door of the pantry and looked out that window. "Yeah, it sure looks like Big Blue from here. The lights are up high and running around the cab of the truck. I'll bet it's Nicki driving."

Reno nodded. Nicki always did have a heavy hand

with grinding gears. She'd learned to drive on a tractor. She'd made the gears on their father's truck grind almost the same way. Of course, that'd been fifteen years ago. She was a pretty good driver these days.

Jacob shook his head. "That man must be crazy in love to let his wife drive like that."

"I hear that's the way it is," Brad said. "First they get you all married up, and then look what happens. You can't even drive your own truck."

"Hush about the driving," Chrissy said as she walked back to where everyone else was standing. "I remember Nicki, and she wouldn't be driving that way, either, unless something was wrong."

"I hope no one's hurt." Reno had looked out for his sister all his life. He felt a sudden guilt that he'd hardly thought about her much at all since that letter had arrived at the post office in Dry Creek. He hadn't even called Nicki and Garrett when they were down in Denver. Of course, they hadn't called him either.

The sound of the truck was louder now that it was turning into the yard of the Redfern Ranch.

"Well, no point in us standing here wondering about it. Let's step outside and see what's going on," Jacob said as he walked toward the door.

"Let me put Justin in his crib," Reno said. No one knew for sure it was Nicki and Garrett out there, and Reno wasn't taking any chances. He turned to Chrissy. "Is there a rattle or something that he likes to play with so he doesn't cry?"

"Justin hardly ever cries," Chrissy protested.

Jacob and the other two men walked out on the porch.

"I know," Reno said as he handed Justin into Chrissy's arms. "It's just that now would be a very good time for him to be quiet so that no one knows he's here."

"Oh," Chrissy said. "Sorry. I wasn't thinking."

"It's Nicki," Jacob called from outside.

Chrissy stood on the side of the porch. She had laid Justin down inside in his crib, and she could hear him from the porch. She had thought about wrapping the baby up in his blanket and taking him out with her to greet Nicki and Garrett, but something stopped her.

Chrissy realized Nicki and Garrett didn't know she was here. She was sure of Garrett's welcome, but not of Nicki's. Nicki had seemed very friendly when Chrissy was here before, but Chrissy figured there was a difference between being friendly to someone who was staying for only a few days and someone who looked as if they had moved into your bunkhouse.

Reno knew something was wrong the minute his sister stepped down out of the cab of her husband's truck. For one thing, she didn't appear to have her husband with her. For another thing, she didn't appear to have much of her hair, either.

"Welcome home, sis," Reno said as he stepped

forward to welcome Nicki with a big hug. Nicki had never paid much attention to fashion before she got married, but even then she'd never had her hair in a short, shaggy, bizarre cut like this with one side shorter than the other. "It's good to have you back."

Nicki walked into his arms before she started to sob.

"It's just horr—horren—awful," Nicki wailed.

Jacob and the two ranch hands milled around with their hands in their pockets. Reno could see they wanted to be helpful but weren't sure what was wrong.

"I guess this isn't them guys you were worried about earlier at least," Mark, the quiet ranch hand, finally said. "That's good. No need to worry."

Nicki pulled herself back from Reno's arms and took a deep breath. "I'm sorry if I worried you driving in like that. It's just that I've had a—" Nicki took a deep breath "—a horrendous experience." Nicki smiled at Reno to show she'd learned yet another word.

"Was it lice?" Jacob asked in concern.

"What?"

"I thought it might be lice on account of the way you've chopped off your hair."

"My hair happens to be the latest fashion you can find in Denver," Nicki said with her chin in the air. "It is not odd—or even unusual I think is the word Garrett used."

"So you cut it that way on purpose?" Jacob asked.

"Nicki looks great in any hairstyle," Reno said swiftly, with a look at Jacob to let him know that the haircut had, obviously, been intentional.

"Thank you." Nicki smiled. "I knew you would stand by me even when Garrett wouldn't."

"Wait a minute." Reno didn't want to take sides in a marital argument, not that he wasn't surprised that Nicki and Garrett were even having an argument. It must be a first for them. "I'm not sure now's the time—"

"Oh," Nicki gasped as she took another step back and looked at Reno more closely. "I didn't notice. Did someone die? Oh, my, it wasn't anyone I know, was it?"

"Of course no one died."

"Then why are you wearing your suit?" Nicki asked. "You shouldn't scare a person like that. I thought you had been to a funeral."

Brad started to chuckle. "No, ma'am, he was just dancing, is all."

"Dancing?" Nicki looked as startled as she would have if someone *had* died. "Here?" Nicki looked around the yard. "There's no place here to dance."

"There's the bunkhouse," Jacob offered.

"Oh, I get it," Nicki finally said. "You're practicing a skit for something. Like the time Lester dressed up like Elvis and paraded into the café. That was a good one. So who are you guys going to be? The Three Stooges?''

''It's not a crime to learn how to dance,'' Reno said. He didn't like the looks that were developing on the faces of Brad and Mark. They hadn't liked being compared to the Three Stooges.

''Ladies like a man who can dance,'' Brad said stiffly.

''I just want to have some fun at the next wedding,'' Mark added.

''Oh.'' Nicki thought for a minute. ''Yeah, that makes sense. What—do you have some kind of an instructional video or something? You could use the VCR at our house if you want.''

''We don't need a VCR,'' Jacob said. ''We have us a dance instructor.''

''A pretty one, too,'' Brad said with more confidence.

Reno could see Nicki running through all the pretty women in Dry Creek and deciding against each one. He might as well come out with it. ''Chrissy Hamilton is here.''

Nicki looked around again.

''In the bunkhouse,'' Reno said.

''Well, why didn't you say so?'' Nicki asked. She sounded as if she had forgotten all about her hair. ''Does she have the baby with her? I told Garrett she didn't need to keep it a secret. I've been dying to see her and the baby! How are they?'' She turned to

Reno. "You know, I think I'm second cousin to Chrissy. Isn't that something? I always thought you and I would have such fun with a cousin, and now we have one."

"She's not *my* cousin," Reno said. "You're the one who married her cousin. Not me."

Reno could have saved his words. No one seemed to care whether or not he was Chrissy's cousin except him. Nicki had already started walking down to the bunkhouse, and Jacob and the two ranch hands were still looking confused.

"Wonder why she'd do that to her hair?" Jacob finally asked.

"What I wonder is where she left that husband of hers," Brad said. "Do you think this means she's single again?"

"Of course not," Reno snapped. He should get down to the bunkhouse, but he didn't want to leave any confusion in Brad's mind. "Married people have arguments. It doesn't mean they're divorced."

"Oh, I know that," Brad said cheerfully. "I was just thinking that if she was to leave that man of hers, she might like some sympathy. I could take her dancing."

"She doesn't dance," Reno said as he started to walk away.

"I can teach her," Brad called after him. "Now that I've been taught myself, I can teach anyone."

"She's still married!" Reno shouted back.

One thing he knew for sure was that Nicki would never divorce her husband. Once she was married, she was married. Reno was like her in that regard. They'd both seen the pain of a divorce. Maybe that's why it had taken them both so long to think about getting married.

Chapter Thirteen

Chrissy gave up trying to get Justin to sleep. First Nicki had come down to the bunkhouse in a whirlwind of kisses and excitement. And then Reno had joined them just as Nicki mentioned that she should go up to the main house to see if there were any phone messages for her on the answering machine.

"Come with me?" Nicki asked.

Chrissy propped Justin up against her shoulder. That made him stop squirming, at least. "Of course. Do you think Garrett will call?"

Nicki had told Chrissy a little of their argument before Reno came into the room.

"Oh, I'm not waiting for Garrett's call," Nicki said with an unconvincing smile. "I'm curious about whether that order for cattle feed I called in before I left is finally ready to be picked up at the hardware store.''

''I'm sure Jacob would have mentioned it,'' Reno said.

Chrissy frowned at Reno. Sometimes, she thought, men could be so dense. ''It's worth checking anyway.''

''Sure. Why not?'' Reno said as he stepped closer to Chrissy and held out his arms. ''But you better let me carry Justy here across the yard. It's still muddy enough out there to be slippery in places.''

''Justy?''

''I'm trying to find a nickname for him, but I don't think that's it,'' Reno said as he glanced over at the door. ''It's chilly out there, too. Better bring an extra blanket.''

Chrissy held Justin out to him, and the baby went to Reno easily. Weren't babies supposed to cry when you handed them to strangers? she asked herself as she reached over to the bed and grabbed another one of Justin's blankets.

''Oh.'' Nicki stopped as she was walking toward the door and turned back to stare at Reno. ''The baby's not crying or anything. He cried when I picked him up. He likes you.''

''Well, you don't need to sound so surprised,'' Reno said.

''I've just never seen you with a baby before.'' Nicki looked at him.

Chrissy could see where this was headed. They had been down this road before in the past couple of days. "Reno's not the baby's father."

"Well, of course not." Nicki looked startled now. "Who said he was?"

"Oh, I forgot, you didn't see the letter. You must be the only one in Dry Creek who hasn't."

"What letter? Did Reno write you a letter?"

"It's not from Reno. We may as well go up to the other house. I think Reno still has the letter there someplace. You can read it for yourself," Chrissy said as she walked toward the door.

"And take a jacket for yourself, too," Reno called back to Chrissy from the porch. "Use that denim one of mine if you need to—"

"I can use a blanket," Chrissy said. The blankets weren't hers any more than the jacket was, but they felt more like hers, and she wanted to borrow only as much as was absolutely necessary.

Reno and Nicki were waiting for her on the porch. Reno frowned at the blanket, but he didn't say anything. "Here, hold on to one of my arms. You should have worn my extra pair of boots down here. With a couple layers of socks, they would have been fine."

"My shoes are good enough for dancing," Chrissy said as she held on to the elbow he had bent. "Besides, your feet are a size twelve. It'd take more than a couple of pairs of socks to make them fit."

Chrissy had no sooner put her hand in the crook of

Reno's arm than he pulled his arm closer to his side and her hand with it, forcing her to walk even closer to him.

"Well, you can have all my socks, then," Reno said.

Chrissy didn't have the courage to look at Nicki directly, but she did glance over at her. Reno's sister was staring at the two of them as though she'd never seen a man offer a woman his entire sock wardrobe before.

"I'm going to buy some boots with my first check," Chrissy said to Nicki, hoping it would help. "It's not like I'm a complete charity case."

"Well, of course not," Nicki said decisively as she finally started to walk toward the house. "I forgot. Reno always helps family."

Chrissy nodded. She had suspected as much. Garrett would have helped her, too.

The walk across the yard wasn't nearly long enough for Reno. The night had turned a little warmer than it had been when he was outside rocking Justin earlier, and Reno liked the feel of Chrissy's hand tucked close to his side. With Justin in his arms and Chrissy walking close to him, he was a contented man.

The night was dark except for the yard light.

"I'll go ahead and open the door," Nicki said. She was already ahead of them in her walk across the yard.

"Put some water on for tea, too," Reno called after her.

"Tea?" Nicki turned back. "Since when do you drink tea?"

"Since coffee isn't good for Chrissy. Not now with the baby," Reno answered.

"Oh," Nicki said as she started up the steps of the main house.

"You don't have to drink tea because of me," Chrissy said.

"A man never died from drinking a cup of tea," Reno said. You would think it was a crime to change a habit, the way Nicki was looking at him tonight. It did a man good to change his ways every now and again.

"Here, watch this step," Reno said when they came to the porch.

Nicki had turned the light on in the kitchen by the time Reno and Chrissy came inside. Reno had thought Nicki's hair was an odd color when he'd seen it down in the bunkhouse, yet he hadn't been sure because the light wasn't very good down there. But under the kitchen light her hair looked almost orange. Of course, it was hard to tell, because it was so short.

"Now, where's the teakettle?" Nicki said as she walked over to the old stove. "Ah, there it is. Just give me a second to light a match, and we'll have it all set."

"Light a match?" Chrissy asked.

Nicki looked at Reno and Chrissy. "Which one of you is doing the cooking these days?"

"Men can cook," Reno said. "You don't need to assume that just because Chrissy is a woman she's doing the cooking."

Nicki shrugged as she picked up the teakettle and walked over to the sink. "I'm just surprised she likes your fried potatoes that well, that's all."

"We haven't had fried potatoes," Chrissy said.

"Well, then, what's he been feeding you?" Nicki asked as turned on the water and filled up the teakettle.

"We've had meat loaf," Reno said. "With baked potatoes."

Reno didn't add that Mrs. Hargrove had written down the recipe for baked potatoes when she slipped a couple of potatoes into the sack that held a piece of her foil-wrapped meat loaf.

"And canned corn," Chrissy added. "It was all very good."

Nicki brought the teakettle back to the stove. "Sounds good to me."

"We have to have good meals for Chrissy." Reno defended himself, even though his sister hadn't said anything more. "Because of Justin."

Nicki struck a match and lit a burner on the gas stove. "We should all eat good meals. It keeps a body healthy."

Nicki set the teakettle on the burner. "Now, while

this water gets hot, I think I'll go into the living room and listen to the messages.''

Reno watched his sister leave the kitchen. By now he'd realized that the message she wanted to check for must be from Garrett, and he wanted to give her the privacy she needed.

''I wonder what they fought about,'' Chrissy whispered when Nicki left the room.

''I thought she already told you,'' Reno whispered back. He could hear the soft mumble of the answering machine playing back messages.

Chrissy shook her head. ''She kind of left that part out. Mostly she just said Garrett didn't like her hair.''

''Yeah, that's probably not enough of a reason for this bad of a fight,'' Reno agreed. ''Garrett seems like the kind of a guy who could get used to any kind of hair.''

''Oh, Nicki doesn't like her hair either,'' Chrissy said. ''She already asked me if I can fix it for her.''

Reno would never understand women. ''Well, if she doesn't like her hair, why does she get so upset if someone else says something about it?''

''I think it's just Garrett who upset her.''

The mumble of the answering machine stopped, and both Reno and Chrissy became still.

They didn't even bother to look uninterested when Nicki came back to the kitchen.

''Well,'' Reno asked, ''was there a message for you?''

Nicki shook her head as she held out a small sheet of notepaper. "Not for me. But a Mrs. Bard called. She said something about being very sorry for hiring some attorney and that she wanted you to know she was telling him to stop everything he was doing." Nicki held out the piece of paper. "She left her number and said she'd be very happy if you'd call so she could say how sorry she was to you in person. Although she also said she'd understand if you didn't want to."

"Mrs. Bard called?" Chrissy was still taking it in. "Are you sure it was Mrs. Bard?"

"That's who she said she was. The message is still there, if you'd like to replay it."

Reno was standing. "Thanks for saving it. I think we would like to listen to it again."

Chrissy nodded. "I can't believe she'd call. Not now."

Reno knew what she meant. He couldn't believe it either. He wondered how long Chrissy would stay now that she would feel safe in leaving.

Chrissy sliced a red bell pepper into thin strips. Nicki was chopping onions, and Linda was peeling some cloves of garlic. They were all standing around the counter in the kitchen of the Dry Creek Café. The midday air was sticky and humid. The sky outside was overcast and gray. They had the door to the outside propped open so they could get the breeze.

"Jazz should be here helping," Linda said. "But there's still a lot of mud up on the flats where the Jenkins place is, and he can't get out unless he drives the old tractor the Jenkinses left when they moved to Florida."

"And if it rains again today—which I think it will—he won't get out even with the tractor. The rain always hits that area the worst, and it feels to me like thunderstorm weather today." Nicki blinked. She had been blinking more and more as she cut the onions, but so far Chrissy hadn't seen any tears. Nicki looked over at Linda. "But don't worry. We'll get by without him just fine. I kind of like chopping these onions."

"Besides, aren't you mad at him?" Chrissy asked.

Linda's lips formed a thin line. "Mad or not, he should be here. He's just lucky that Jacob's nephew stopped in Miles City and picked up the waitress uniforms for tonight, or I'd have to be doing that today. It's too much for one person. We're partners in this café, and this catering job is a first for us. We've never cooked for a hundred people before."

"We'll do fine," Chrissy said to reassure her. "You've got the grill all set up, and the potatoes bake themselves. Besides, people won't even notice the rest of the food once they try this salsa. Once we're finished with the salsa, we're home free."

Chrissy still ached from her night of dancing last night, so she was grateful to stand in one place and slice peppers. She would let Jazz deal with the mud.

Reno had offered to keep Justin with him out at the ranch so Chrissy could help Linda today.

Linda nodded. "I guess the salsa is the only complicated thing. Jacob said a party isn't much of a party without something hot and spicy, so he wanted this salsa even though he can't eat any of it himself on his steak."

Nicki shook her head. "Men."

Chrissy shared a look with Linda. So far, Nicki hadn't really talked about her argument with Garrett, but she certainly was chopping the onions on her cutting board with unusual vigor and blinking her eyes often enough that she could be crying.

"They're just never happy with things the way they are," Nicki continued as she halved a big white onion with a single swipe of her knife. "There's nothing wrong with plain steak."

"I must confess I like a little steak sauce myself," Linda said.

"And I'm going to try the salsa," Chrissy added.

Nicki grunted. "Well, I'll probably try the salsa, too. I have to see how my onions taste."

Chrissy looked at the pile of chopped onions that were in the bowl beside Nicki's cutting board. "If it's any consolation, Garrett usually likes his steak plain."

"Plain," Nicki grunted. "At least it's not red, like everything else he likes."

"Maybe you'd like to talk about what happened?" Chrissy suggested.

"Yeah," Linda agreed softly with a twinkle in her eye. "We're running out of things to chop."

"There's still the chives for the baked potatoes," Nicki said, but then she smiled. "I guess I should just spit it out. It's not such a big thing, really—it's just that when we were in Denver Garrett wanted to test-drive this red convertible. I said it sounded like fun and so we did. But I never thought he'd buy it." Nicki paused. "Can you imagine—a red convertible?"

"That doesn't sound like Garrett," Chrissy said carefully. "Did he ask you if you wanted him to buy it?"

"Well, of course, but I said yes," Nicki snapped. This time a tear did roll down her cheek, and she swiped at it with her sleeve. "What kind of wife would tell her husband he can't buy something when it's his own money? I didn't earn any of that money. It's his. He can throw it out of an airplane if he wants."

Linda frowned. "So you're worried that he's wasting money?"

"No, I don't care about the money." Nicki paused and turned to look at the other two women directly. "It's just—well, look at me. Am I the kind of woman a man takes riding in a red convertible?"

A thousand light bulbs went off in Chrissy's head. "Is that what happened to your hair?"

Nicki nodded miserably. "I was going to surprise

Garrett and become a blonde. I thought that would fit in with the red convertible. But the beautician did something funny with the color, and we tried to fix it and it didn't work, so I said she should cut it off, and then—'' Nicki gestured to her hair. ''Finally I just left, and she hadn't even finished. Now look at me.''

''It's not so bad,'' Linda said kindly.

''I know some women can carry off the bald look,'' Nicki said with a sigh. ''Maybe I'll have to try that. I think there's some old sheep shears somewhere on the ranch.''

''Don't you dare,'' Chrissy said. ''Besides, I think I can fix it. When we finish getting everything ready for tonight, we'll set you in the chair over there, and I'll go to work.''

''Do you really think you can fix it?'' Nicki asked hopefully.

Chrissy nodded. ''I didn't spend all those years in front of cosmetic counters for nothing. I've been made over so many times I know most of the tricks.''

''Oh, that would be wonderful. I thought about going to a beauty salon, but the only one I know about is Darlene's Place in Miles City.''

''She closed her shop last winter—turned the building into a video arcade,'' Linda said. ''Now that she's retired, she just sits home and collects her quarters. There's no place closer than Billings now. I've been needing a permanent, too, but I don't know where to go.''

"Why, that's wonderful news," Chrissy said.

Both Nicki and Linda looked at her as if she hadn't been listening.

Chrissy smiled. "I'm not telling anyone else yet, but I'm thinking about going to beauty school, so I can open a place in Dry Creek."

"That's great," Linda said. "Women are always asking about a place to get their hair cut. I think you'll have lots of business."

Nicki nodded. "You'll pull in women from east of here, too—it's closer for them than driving to Billings."

"Well, I have to go to beauty school first, so I thought I'd move back to Los Angeles for a few months so I could do that. But don't tell anyone yet. I haven't decided for sure."

Chrissy didn't want to have everyone know her hopes yet, because they still felt so new to her. Besides, staying in Dry Creek was her dream, and she needed to make it happen herself. First she'd go to school. Then she'd see about renting a place to set up her salon. Then—and this was where her dream merged into pure fantasy—she'd see about finding a house for her and Justin to live in. Maybe a house with chipped appliances that required coaxing before they'd work and a hat rack hanging on the kitchen wall that held a dozen green caps, all with bright yellow tractors on them.

Chrissy stopped the dream right there. She was almost seeing the face of the man sitting at the kitchen table, and that would never do. She knew who the man was. That wasn't the problem. The problem was she couldn't love him. If she ever did get married, it would have to be to a man she didn't need. She had done fine without Jared, and if she ever did marry, it would be to someone who would not devastate her when he left. That would never be Reno. She had a feeling that if she ever started loving him, really loving him, she wouldn't be able to go on when he left. And of course he would leave. All men did.

Chrissy looked around. She didn't have to look far to see women who were unhappy in love.

"A woman can care too much, can't she?" Chrissy asked. "I mean, in a relationship with a man."

"She sure can," Nicki said as she cut through the onion on her board. "That's all I've got to say about it."

Linda looked more uncertain. "I guess it depends. You both need to care to make it work. And you both need to be strong to be a team. I mean, you can't just both be off doing your own thing like…" Her voice trailed off. "Like Jazz and me."

Well, that answered Chrissy's question. She didn't want to be crying like that in a month or two.

"Ah, don't worry." Chrissy put her hand on her new friend's shoulder and lied with all her heart. "It'll be all right—someday—somehow…" Finally

Chrissy felt she should tell the truth, so she whispered the last. "Maybe."

A loud clap of thunder sounded outside, and all three women looked toward the door.

"Look at that rain come down," Nicki said.

The rain beat a steady tune on the roof of the café, and one look out the open door showed that it was already making puddles outside.

"Jazz will never get out now," Linda said.

"We'll be fine," Chrissy said.

Chapter Fourteen

Reno held Justin on his lap—and that was no easy task when a dozen grandmothers all wanted to hold the baby. Reno was sitting on a folding chair in the Elkton barn that stood on the edge of town. The barn hadn't been used for years except for town celebrations like this. Reno had his back to the wall and a stack of damp dish towels on his right. Dinner was over and the dancing had started a few minutes ago.

The only reason that no one was pestering Reno to hold Justin right now was that Reno asked anyone who came up to be his substitute at the coffeepot for a few minutes first. So far he had two takers. Even Brad had wanted a turn at baby holding, and was over at the coffeepot now. Reno had poured at least ten big two-gallon pots of coffee, and he wanted to take a few minutes to hold his...partner.

No, Reno thought to himself, that was not the name for Justin that he was looking for, either. The problem was that the one name that kept coming back to his mind was one he couldn't use. He wanted to call Justin "son."

"Yes." Reno lifted Justin up just for the pleasure of hearing the boy squeal in excitement. "You're really something, you know that?"

Justin smiled back at him. Chrissy might say babies that young didn't smile, but Reno refused to believe it. Babies were a lot smarter than people gave them credit for.

They also listened better. Justin had been a very attentive audience this afternoon when Reno had practiced the question he was going to ask Chrissy tonight. The more Reno rehearsed what he was going to say, the more the wild hope grew inside him that maybe Chrissy would agree. After all, he couldn't give her everything. But he could give her some important things. A home. His love.

Reno looked out at the dance floor in the middle of the barn. So far, about a dozen couples were waltzing to the music, but a lot of people were still standing around the edges.

Linda, Nicki and Chrissy had done a great job with the barn. They had green and blue streamers hanging from some rafters and huge birthday banners on one wall. Jazz had driven into town on a tractor just before the whole party started with a gunnysack full of wild roses. They made the whole barn smell sweet.

The night outside was dark, and the rain was finally letting up. There would be plenty of mud to fight when people tried to get home, but for now everything was magical. The night chill made the inside of the barn feel cozy. And with the roses and the sound of the music, it was very nice.

Of course, the barn was not Paris, but Reno figured this was where he'd have to propose. Now that Mrs. Bard had talked to the attorney, Chrissy had no reason to stay in Dry Creek. He needed to ask his question before she thought about leaving. He knew they'd still have issues to resolve even if she said yes, but he trusted God to help them figure everything out.

Reno was not aware that he had sighed until Nicki sat down in the chair next to him. "Poured a lot of coffee already, huh?"

"Yeah," Reno said. "It's not good for people, you know."

Nicki grunted. "I plan to drink a whole pot of it tonight."

"I thought you said Garrett might get here tonight if he drove through."

"Yeah," Nicki said. "That's why I need the coffee."

Reno could see that Nicki's hair looked better. Somehow she'd managed to get it back to her natural color, and now the short tufts were smoothed out so they looked wispy instead of deranged. "Nice hair."

Nicki nodded. "Thanks. Chrissy fixed it."

Reno could already see Chrissy. She'd been coming back and forth between the café and the barn for a while now. But he'd been counting, and this was the last trip.

When Chrissy had said she was going to wear a uniform tonight, he'd thought she was going to pull out the orange dress. But Jacob's nephew had picked up uniforms in Billings, and both Linda and Chrissy looked like French maids, with black dresses and ruffled white aprons.

Reno frowned. Aprons in Dry Creek had never looked like those. That's why Reno knew he needed to time his request for a dance carefully. If he waited too long, Chrissy would be whirled off to dance with someone else. With her hair swept up into that braid she wore, Chrissy was beautiful.

"She's got a way with hair," Nicki offered by way of conversation. "Plus, I like her."

This time Reno was the one to grunt. "I expect she'll be leaving before long."

"Really? She told you about her plans?" Nicki turned to him and asked.

Reno's heart sank. "No, she didn't need to…"

"But—" Nicki began.

"Could you hold Justin for a minute?" Reno interrupted his sister as he stood up. Chrissy had just folded the last tablecloth. Reno turned around and held Justin out to his sister. "If Brad comes back, he's next in line to hold the baby. Right now I've got to do something."

* * *

Chrissy was tired until Reno asked her to dance. "I thought you might want to practice some more. You didn't get your full lesson the other night, because you had to take care of Justin."

When the dancing started, Jazz had hung some brass lanterns with candles in them from the rafters and then turned off the overhead lights. The candlelight and the smell of wild roses turned the barn into a grand ballroom.

Reno guided Chrissy to the quietest corner on the barn floor and started to dance with her.

"You don't need lessons," Chrissy finally whispered as she arched back from Reno so she could see his face better in the shadows. Reno continually surprised her. She had always assumed he was so dedicated to his ranch that he didn't socialize enough to know how to dance like this. But if he danced like this… "You must have been on some pretty fancy dates."

"None that compares with this one." Reno guided her closer to him and started dancing again.

"Oh."

"In fact, I'm thinking it will have to do instead of Paris."

"Oh." Chrissy had a funny feeling in her stomach that was interfering with her breathing. Reno sounded different. As if he was about to make an announcement or something. "Are you planning to fire me?"

"What?" Reno sounded startled.

"Well, I've only been able to feed the calves once

so far, and that's my job. I wouldn't really blame you if you needed to fire me.''

"No one's firing anyone," Reno said firmly. "I don't care about you feeding the calves.''

"Well, but I'm living in the bunkhouse and everything. If you want me to leave, I'd understand.''

Chrissy didn't know why she was rattling on like this. Anyone would think she wanted to be fired. It was just that she was having a hard time thinking. Maybe she was allergic to the roses.

"I don't want you to leave. In fact—" Reno took a deep breath and stopped dancing so he could look down at her "—I want you to stay.''

"Oh.''

"And just so there's no misunderstanding, I'm asking you to marry me.''

Chrissy couldn't breathe. She wondered if she was going to pass out.

Reno paused as if he expected an answer, but when he didn't get one, he started talking again. "I've given it a lot of thought, and there are advantages for you in marrying me. I've got a house and a steady income. Granted, the house needs a new kitchen, but we can work on that. Besides, Justin needs a father, and I'd like to be his father. I could look after both of you, and you wouldn't need to worry.''

"Oh.'' Chrissy found it was remarkably easy to start breathing again. Although she was having some trouble with her vision being blurry. She blinked. "So you want to marry me so you can take care of me and Justin.''

Reno nodded in relief. "Yes."

"I'm sorry, I can't," Chrissy said as she blinked again. "It's kind of you, but I don't take charity."

"It's not—" Reno started to say, but Chrissy had already turned to walk away. She needed a breath of fresh air. It was the roses. That's what it was. She really must be allergic. It was affecting her eyes and everything. She kept her head down as she walked toward the door.

Reno decided he'd lied to himself all night. He'd told himself he was prepared for Chrissy to say no, but he wasn't. He'd had to ask, but he'd never reconcile himself to her answer.

The chatter of the couples talking as they danced and the sounds of someone moving a tray of coffee cups slowly filtered into Reno's mind. Chrissy had gone toward the door so fast she hadn't seen that Garrett had stepped through it only minutes before she had.

Reno heard Garrett call Chrissy's name, but he could see she didn't stop.

And now Garrett was frowning and walking toward Reno.

"What'd you do to upset my cousin?" Garrett demanded when he finally stood before Reno. "She's crying."

Reno looked over at Garrett. His new brother-in-law looked as if he hadn't slept in days and hadn't smiled in even longer. The man was itching for a fight.

"Probably the same thing you did to upset my sister," Reno said as he braced his feet so he could take a punch if one was coming. He figured he could give Garrett as good as he got if it came to fists.

Garrett's anger deflated. "I don't know what I did to upset your sister."

Reno relaxed his muscles. "Yeah, well, I don't know, either."

The other couples on the dance floor danced around Reno and Garrett as if they were part of the decorations.

Garrett shook his head. "I don't think I understand women very much."

Reno grunted. "Welcome to the club."

Garrett was silent.

"I think it was something about her hair," Garrett said finally. "All I said was that it was sure short." Garrett paused. "And a little orange."

"Yeah, well, all I said was that if Chrissy was with me, she wouldn't need to worry," Reno said.

"Worry about what?" Garrett looked up. "Is something happening? She got this strange message on the answer machine at the ranch house from a Mrs. Bard saying that the attorney hadn't been able to get his message through and that she should be careful."

Time froze for Reno. "You mean tonight?"

Garrett nodded. "I thought Nicki might have left

me a message, so I stopped at your house to see. I didn't actually listen to the message. Mrs. Bard was leaving it when I was there, and I overheard it."

"So she just left the message?"

"What does it mean?"

"It means we keep our eyes open and hope we don't see a black strange car around here." Reno looked over at the people by the coffee table. He saw Nicki talking with Mrs. Hargrove, but neither one of them had Justin in their arms.

"That wouldn't be a fairly new black car with tinted windows? Four doors? Rides low like it's been modified somehow?"

Reno's attention came back fully to Garrett.

Garrett continued, "I saw a car like that when I was starting up the road to the ranch. It was coming out. I thought maybe someone had been to visit you and found you weren't home."

Reno started to walk across the room, and Garrett followed. Something about them made the couples stop dancing as the two men walked through.

"What's wrong?" someone said.

Reno didn't turn back to answer whoever had asked the question. He was close enough to Nicki to ask his own question. "Where's Justin?"

Nicki looked up. "Brad has him, remember? It was his turn to hold him."

Reno looked up and down the people sitting in the row of chairs on the side of the barn. He didn't see Brad.

"Brad! Brad Parker!" Reno turned and called.

"Yeah, what's the matter?" Brad stepped out of the circle of people who had been dancing. He had his arm around one of the Baldwin girls.

"Where's Justin?"

"Oh, I gave him to the next guy on the list."

Reno's heart stopped. "What guy? What's his name?"

"I don't know his name. He was hanging around the coffee table after you started dancing, and when I said I was in line to hold Justin, he said he was next."

"You gave a baby to a man, and you didn't even know the man's name!" Reno knew half the reason he was so angry was that he shouldn't have left Justin himself. No matter what it took, Reno should have held him all night.

"Well, the girls were all coming over to see the baby, and we got to talking and then I thought I should dance with at least one of them and—" Brad slowed down and swallowed. "I'm sorry. I thought you weren't worried about those bad guys anymore."

"Did you see where he went?" Reno asked, and then turned to face the rest of his neighbors. "Did anyone see where the man went who was holding the baby?"

Reno heard a gasp by the doorway and looked up. Chrissy was standing there, white-faced and still. How was he ever going to face her? He'd just told her she wouldn't have to worry if she stayed with him, and look what had happened!

One of the ranch hands standing by the door cleared his throat. He'd just come in from the porch. "I saw a man with a baby get into a black car a little bit ago."

"Which way did he go?"

"He headed east from here, but then he took a turn up toward the flats." The ranch hand coughed. "I noticed it because I knew he'd be back in no time. A car like that will never make it through the mud up there."

"That's for sure. I can't get through that mud in my pickup," another man said.

"My tractor will make it through," Jazz said. He was standing quietly beside Reno. "That's why I drove it in instead of my pickup. That old tractor will go anywhere up there, even off the road if you need."

Reno nodded. "Let's go."

Reno's eyes were still on Chrissy. She looked as if she was going to faint.

"I'm in," Garrett said as he stepped next to Reno, and then looked at the ranch hand who'd seen the car leave. "How many guys were in that car?"

"Just two of them," said the ranch hand who'd seen the car leave.

"I'll come, too," Jazz said. "In case the tractor starts acting funny."

Reno caught Mrs. Hargrove's eye and silently mouthed the words asking her to go stand beside

Chrissy. The older woman hadn't taught Sunday school for all those years without being able to read lips in a crowd. She nodded when she understood, and started walking over to Chrissy.

"Here, take some of these," Nicki said.

Reno turned his gaze back just as Nicki handed him a bunch of long barbecue forks. They'd used them in grilling the steaks.

"Those guys might be armed," Nicki explained.

Jazz turned a little white. "I hope they don't have guns."

"Those forks are pretty sturdy," Nicki said as she bent one slightly and nodded in satisfaction. "Sturdy and sharp. A poke with one of these would let someone know you're serious."

Reno took the forks. He didn't have time to argue. He started walking toward the door. Garrett followed.

Nicki nodded. "I'm taking one of the forks for me, too."

"Where do you think you're going?" Garrett, turning back, demanded to know.

"I know those flats better than any of you," Nicki said as she started toward the door, too. "I ride my horse there all the time. Besides, I know how to stand on a tractor without falling off."

"You can fall off a tractor?" Garrett sounded surprised. They were at the door now. "Maybe we should take my car."

Nicki grunted. "That little tin can convertible wouldn't make it past the first turn."

"I thought you were the one who wanted that convertible," Garrett said. "If you didn't like it, why didn't you say so?"

Chrissy watched all four of them walk out the door. Mrs. Hargrove had her arm around Chrissy and she felt some of the chill leaving her. Chrissy took a deep breath. She had to think. "I need to go get Justin."

Mrs. Hargrove squeezed her shoulders. "I don't know if there's even room for all four of them on that tractor. They can't take any more people."

"I'm not going with them," Chrissy announced. She should never have allowed herself to get soft. Since she'd been in Dry Creek, she'd forgotten her own rule. She could depend only on herself. That was the way it had been all her life and that was the way it was now. She'd have to go for Justin.

"But there's no way to get a car or a truck up on those flats. Jazz is right about that," Mrs. Hargrove said gently.

"Then I'll walk," Chrissy said. Yes, the warmth was returning to her arms. She felt as if she could do anything she had to do. "Reno has some old boots in his pickup that he uses in the mud. I'll put them on and walk up there."

Mrs. Hargrove nodded as though she was thinking. "All right. Then I'm coming with you."

"But you can't—" Chrissy stopped short of offending Mrs. Hargrove. "I mean, it's a long way over to those flats, and it's not good for everyone to get that kind of exercise.''

Mrs. Hargrove stood up straight. ''I may be old, but I'm in good physical shape. Besides, you'll need someone to show you the way, and the only one who knows those flats better than Nicki is me. I used to live up there years ago.''

Chrissy nodded. She could use a guide. ''Then I'll pay you, of course.''

''What?'' Mrs. Hargrove looked even more offended than she had when Chrissy had suggested she was old.

''That's the way it has to be,'' Chrissy said. ''I take care of my own.''

Mrs. Hargrove pursed her lips. ''We'll talk about it later.''

Since they were both already standing close to the door, it was a simple thing to slip out without anyone seeing them leave. Everyone else had crowded toward the middle of the barn, exchanging stories about seeing the man in the black car and wondering if they should call the sheriff.

The boots were cold, but Reno had a couple of jackets in his pickup, as well. Chrissy slipped one over her maid's uniform and handed one to Mrs. Hargrove.

''I don't suppose we should take a wrench or anything,'' Chrissy said. ''With all this talk of weapons, I'm wondering if we should have something with us to help.''

"God is our help," Mrs. Hargrove announced decisively as she stepped away from the pickup and pointed herself toward the flats.

"Well, I'll just have to pay Him, too," Chrissy said before she realized she'd spoken aloud.

Fortunately, this time Mrs. Hargrove wasn't offended. In fact, she laughed. "You sound like you're not used to accepting help from anyone."

"I'm not," Chrissy said as she started to walk. She could see the outline of the tractor as it moved up the road. "It's always been just me and my mother."

Mrs. Hargrove nodded as she matched her steps to Chrissy's. "And now it's just you and Justin."

"Yes," Chrissy said. She swallowed a sob. "Just the two of us."

Chapter Fifteen

Chrissy had cold gray mud on her arms and her legs and her face. And if that wasn't bad enough, she had slid down the latest slope and was now sitting in mud. It had stopped raining completely since she and Mrs. Hargrove had walked out of Dry Creek. After it stopped raining, a half-moon appeared in the sky. When they started out, they could find their way only because they could see the fence posts that lined the land on the flats. Now the moon gave them some light, unless it went behind a cloud.

"Well, at least we know we're on the right road," Chrissy said as she put her hand down to give herself leverage to stand. "I can see the wheel prints from the tractor when I'm down here."

"That's good." Mrs. Hargrove turned to look down the road. "I expect they've already gotten to

Justin. I keep thinking we should see some lights from the tractor.''

"How much farther to where Justin is?" Chrissy said as she stood. She knew Mrs. Hargrove didn't know the answer, but she just wanted to hear her say some more reassuring words.

Mrs. Hargrove had stopped to pray periodically as they walked, and each time the older woman thanked God for the tractor and for a strong young man like Reno to go after Justin. Chrissy relaxed more and more each time the older woman prayed. Mrs. Hargrove prayed with such conviction Chrissy almost came to believe it would be all right.

"Well, I don't know." Mrs. Hargrove smiled. "Maybe it's not as close as you'd like. But don't worry. It's in God's hands. And remember, we've both agreed that no one would hurt Justin. They must have orders not to hurt him.''

Mrs. Hargrove had led the way for a long time now, and Chrissy had followed.

"I never should have let you come out here," Chrissy said. "But I'm so glad you did. I would have been crazy by now, and you keep reminding me that Justin will be all right.''

Mrs. Hargrove nodded. "It's good to have someone help you over the rough patches.''

"I—'' Chrissy started to repeat the phrase she must have said a dozen times tonight. She knew now the words weren't true. "I guess I do need the help of others sometimes."

"We all do," Mrs. Hargrove said as she started walking forward. "That's what makes a church."

"There's not a church out here, is there?" Chrissy peered into the darkness. She'd be grateful for some steps to sit on for a minute or two.

"No." Mrs. Hargrove chuckled. "I mean the people part of the church."

"I haven't actually gone to the church yet," Chrissy cautioned the older woman.

"But you will," Mrs. Hargrove said. "In your time."

"Maybe," Chrissy said as she matched the older woman's steps. Something about the darkness made it easy to talk to Mrs. Hargrove. "Reno asked me to marry him tonight."

"Ah." The older woman stopped and looked at Chrissy.

Chrissy shrugged. "He doesn't love me or anything like that. He just wants to take care of me and Justin."

"I see." Mrs. Hargrove started to walk again.

Chrissy thought she saw a small smile on the woman's face in the moonlight, but she must have been mistaken. The moonlight was gone almost as soon as it appeared, and when Chrissy looked again there was no smile.

"I guess that's why he would want to take care of

us, huh?'' Chrissy said. ''Sort of a mission for the church.''

''Oh, I doubt it's that. Not if I know Reno,'' Mrs. Hargrove said.

''Well, he is awfully fond of Justin.''

''And I've seen how he looks at you.''

Chrissy didn't answer. Mrs. Hargrove was right about a lot of things, but not about this. ''All I know is that the more he wants to give me, the more nervous I get. Why—he even wanted to give me his socks! All of them.''

''That is an unusual gift,'' Mrs. Hargrove agreed.

''Well, it was so I could wear a pair of his boots and not have to worry about ruining my shoes in the mud.''

''I see. Very sensible of him, then,'' Mrs. Hargrove said as she peered ahead. ''I think I see a light.''

Reno peered into the darkness. The tractor pulled and groaned as it crawled ahead. Its headlights didn't shine too far into the night, so Reno had to squint and pray to keep on the old road. Of course, the tractor wasn't made for taking a midnight drive. Most ranchers didn't drive their tractors anywhere at night except maybe out to their fields.

Still, even as hard as it was to see, Reno was a happy man. There was a thick chain stretched out behind the tractor, and at the end of the chain was a late-model black car.

Inside the car, Jazz sat in the driver's seat where he could keep an eye on one of the gentlemen who used to drive the black car. Reno used the term "gentlemen" loosely. What he really meant was that the two men had obligingly worn expensive silk ties with their equally expensive suits. The ties made it so much easier to keep the two men's hands firmly behind their backs. The other man was in the back seat squeezed between the door and Garrett. On the other side of Garrett sat Nicki, holding Justin.

Not only was Justin well, the baby seemed to think they were taking him on this outing for his pleasure.

Fortunately, the thick mud had so thoroughly discouraged the kidnappers that Reno thought they were almost happy to see them coming. The two had both been outside the car looking and pointing at their wheels that were buried halfway up the hubcaps in mud.

Well, the kidnappers had been relieved until Nicki jumped off the tractor and pointed two of her barbecue forks at them. They'd looked a little startled then, and one of them offered to turn in the attorney to make a better deal for himself.

Reno had assured them both they would meet with the law soon enough and that they could propose their deals at that time.

Reno turned around to look behind him. He could see Garrett and Nicki talking in the back seat of the car, and it didn't look like they were arguing. That was a good thing. Nicki deserved a happy marriage.

Reno had held Justin for a long minute after he pulled him out of the black car and scolded the kidnappers for not having an infant car seat.

"Yeah, well, those babies are nothing but a big pain," one of the kidnappers had said. "They don't care if you're the one in charge."

Reno realized he was going to miss having a baby around. He couldn't picture himself married if it wasn't going to be to Chrissy, so he'd never have any children of his own. Reno decided it was a good thing Nicki had gotten married, so he could at least have some nieces and nephews.

Reno had been lost in thought, so it took a moment to figure out that there was some white thing flapping in the darkness ahead. Of all the peculiar things. It looked as if some cowboy had left a white apron on the fence along the road. Reno leaned farther forward. No, that couldn't be right. The apron looked to be moving like a flag.

Chrissy watched the tractor come into view, and she saw the car that it pulled. "Is Justin all right?"

Chrissy knew her voice was loud, but she didn't expect the tractor to jerk to a stop at the sound of her voice or for Reno to climb down off the tractor and take such huge strides toward her and Mrs. Hargrove.

"Yes, he's fine." Reno stopped when he was about

three feet away. "But what are the two of you doing out here?"

"Strolling out to meet you," Mrs. Hargrove said, just as if anyone could stroll in this kind of mud. "It's kind of you to stop for us."

"Stop for you?" Reno seemed dumbfounded. "Of course I'm stopping for you. You're in the middle of nowhere. There aren't even cows out this far! I thought the two of you must be a mirage."

"Doesn't that only happen in the desert?" Mrs. Hargrove asked.

"It *should* only happen in the desert," Reno agreed. "But nothing seems to be happening right tonight."

"Well, we don't know that, do we? The night's not over yet," Mrs. Hargrove said as she walked toward the car. "Do you suppose there's room for me in there?"

"I don't know," Reno said. "There's five people already. Six with Justin. I guess we could get two more in."

Mrs. Hargrove bent to look in the window that Jazz had rolled down. "Hi, everyone. Mind if we hitch a ride?"

Chrissy walked over to the window, too.

"Of course not," Nicki said as she opened the back door next to where she was sitting.

"Justin!" Chrissy cried out as she held out her arms for her baby.

Nicki lifted the baby up to her.

Reno joined everyone by the window and frowned. "I don't know if we're going to have room for everyone inside."

"Oh, well, Chrissy is too muddy to ride in here anyway," Mrs. Hargrove said. "She'd ruin the seats."

Mrs. Hargrove, Chrissy and Reno were all standing around the one open window.

"Oh, I can put a blanket under me." Chrissy looked up from her baby. "It'll be fine."

"But it's such a nice night out," Mrs. Hargrove continued. "And you've never had a tractor ride before. This is your chance."

"I'm not sure—" Reno started before Mrs. Hargrove stepped on his foot.

"Chrissy would like to take a tractor ride, wouldn't you?" Mrs. Hargrove said.

"Uh, yeah. Sure," Chrissy said.

Reno didn't have to look at Chrissy's face to know that she was just being polite. It was hard to say no to Mrs. Hargrove. Chrissy bent to give Justin back to Nicki.

"It's kind of bumpy," Reno warned her.

Mrs. Hargrove stepped on his foot again. Reno figured he better shut up if he wanted to keep his toes.

Chrissy started walking toward the tractor.

"What do you think you're doing?" Reno turned to whisper to the older woman.

"Just be charming," Mrs. Hargrove hissed back as she started bending to sit inside the car. "I must say, you used to be better at this in the first grade."

Chrissy decided they should outlaw tractors. She'd never realized there was nowhere for a passenger to sit on a tractor. At first she thought she could stand on that big round thing that went between the wheels. That was what she climbed on to wait for Reno.

Reno climbed up on the other side of the tractor. "You'll fall off if you stay there."

Chrissy looked around. Reno had left the lights going on the tractor, but they gave more of a soft glow than any kind of real light. "Don't they have some kind of fold-down seat for passengers?"

Reno grunted. "They have one seat. Made out of tin. And it bounces."

"Well, where did Nicki sit?"

"Nicki likes to ride the wheel." Reno sat down in the one seat and pointed to the huge metal piece that rose out above the big tires. "But that's an acquired skill. I wouldn't recommend it for your first tractor ride."

"Well, where *would* you recommend?"

Reno bent and adjusted the metal seat so it moved back a few inches and then patted his knee. "Here."

"On your lap?" Chrissy swallowed. "But I'm all muddy."

"Mud doesn't bother me." Reno remembered it

was mud that Chrissy thought was keeping her out of the car. "In fact, I've grown fond of mud lately."

"You're sure?" Chrissy asked as she slid toward him.

"I see you have my boots on." Reno knew the importance of talking softly to someone who was nervous.

"I hope you don't mind," Chrissy said as she put her foot on the floor beneath Reno's foot.

"Not at all." Reno held out his hands and lifted Chrissy onto his lap. "Did you remember to use extra socks?"

Chrissy shook her head. "I think that's why I'm getting a blister."

"Oh, well," Reno said as he felt Chrissy start to relax on his lap. "You'll remember next time."

Reno didn't need to start the tractor again, but he did need to put it in gear to move forward. He thought they were about a mile off the main road into Dry Creek. It could take the old tractor ten minutes to go a mile if he kept it in first gear.

Reno drove the tractor with one hand and kept the other hand around Chrissy's back.

"I'm sorry I didn't watch over Justin better." Reno didn't know how to say it other than to say it straight out. "If anything had happened to him, I would never have forgiven myself."

"I know."

"I wouldn't blame you if you never trusted me with another thing."

Reno couldn't see Chrissy's eyes because of the darkness, but he could see the slight smile that moved her lips in the light of the half-moon.

"Oh. Well, I was going to ask you to help me with a few things," Chrissy finally said.

"Really?" Reno knew Chrissy never asked anyone for help. If he hadn't been so surprised, he would have answered her sooner. He didn't realize the pause was long until he felt some stiffness in her back.

"That is, if you're willing to help me," she added.

"Of course I'll help you." Reno felt her back relax.

"You haven't even asked what it is."

"I don't need to know. You'll tell me when you're ready."

The tractor growled low and deep as it moved toward the main road. Reno tried to think of something charming to say. Why was it that when he most wanted to say something compelling, he had no words at all?

"I was thinking," Chrissy said hesitantly.

"Yes?"

"Well, if you were to help me with a few things, would that be enough? I mean, I don't think you should marry someone just so you can be there to take care of them."

"What?" Reno growled in rhythm with the tractor.

"I didn't ask you to marry me just so I could take care of you…"

"Oh?"

Reno took a deep breath and forced his voice into a whisper. "I asked you to marry me because I love you."

"Oh."

Reno wasn't sure, but he thought *that* "oh" sounded a little happier. "I don't have much to offer except my love and the ranch, but that's what I meant to say."

Reno figured he would spend the rest of his life thinking of more charming ways to say what he was about to say. "Since I didn't make it clear the first time, I'm going to ask again. Chrissy Hamilton, will you marry me?"

"Maybe."

"Maybe?" Reno ground the word out as the tractor pulled into Dry Creek. "What do you mean 'maybe'?"

Although the windows in the houses of Dry Creek were all dark, someone in the barn saw them coming down the road and shouted out that they were back. But Reno wasn't paying any attention. The night was just light enough he could see Chrissy smile as she said, "Well, probably. But I have a few things to do first. Can you wait?"

"I'll wait all my life if I need to."

Reno figured he had just enough time to kiss Chrissy before the whole town descended upon them.

Epilogue

Six months later

A few snowflakes fell here and there on the main road in Dry Creek, but winter was only beginning and it was still warm enough to be outside, especially if a man—or a woman—had a cap on.

Reno and Chrissy were both wearing green tractor caps, even though, as Chrissy said, they should upgrade to a big-league sports cap now that she'd become a licensed beautician.

Reno disagreed. He said tractors had served them well.

What could Chrissy do but smile and agree?

Chrissy was a happy woman. She and Reno were leaning against the hood of his pickup and looking through the big window into the Dry Creek hardware store. The pickup was parked far enough away that the people inside the hardware store didn't see them watching.

Not that they would have cared. She and Reno had waited inside for a little while for the mail to be delivered and then decided to wait outside where they could be together. Only Mrs. Hargrove knew they had left the store, and that was because she was the one holding Justin.

Reno had leaned against the pickup first and then opened his arms so that Chrissy could lean against his chest instead of the cold metal of the pickup hood.

"I still mean to take you to Paris someday," Reno whispered in her ear once Chrissy had settled against him.

"Someday," Chrissy agreed as she looked down the street to see if the mailman was coming.

She didn't see the mailman's truck, but she did let her eyes linger on the church building. She sometimes wondered these days why it had taken her so long to accept that God cared about her. And not just God; other people cared, too. She was so well loved, she no longer tried to do everything herself. Not that she wanted to be dependent, either. She still planned to open that beauty salon and have her own business. Reno was her biggest supporter in that dream.

"Here he comes," Reno said softly in her ear.

"I wonder if it will be here today."

"We mailed it in Billings yesterday. It should be here.''

The mailman drove his truck next to the door of the hardware store and parked. He picked up a leather bag full of mail before stepping out of the truck and walking up the steps. The man looked as if he was in his usual hurry, and he pulled out several banded packets of mail and set them on the counter inside the hardware store before placing one single letter on top of all the bundles.

Chrissy smiled. Jacob was sorting the mail again, and he held the first envelope up and stared at it for a minute. Then he called over to Elmer. In the meantime, Lester came over to look at the envelope. Lester gestured for Mrs. Hargrove to come. With everyone gathering around the envelope, Glory and Pastor Matthew came over, too.

Finally there were so many people standing around and staring at the envelope that Reno and Chrissy could no longer actually see it.

"Who do you think will open it first?" Reno asked.

"Mrs. Hargrove," Chrissy said. "She'll figure it out in a minute or two."

Mrs. Hargrove didn't actually open the envelope herself, because she had Justin in her arms, but Chrissy could see her urging Jacob to do it. Finally Jacob tore the end off the envelope and pulled out the paper.

Jacob waved everyone away from him so he'd have space in which to read the letter aloud to them.

Chrissy heard Reno whisper the words along with Jacob as the older man read them inside. "Reno Redfern and Christine Hamilton cordially invite all of their friends and neighbors to attend their wedding this coming Christmas Eve in the sanctuary of the Dry Creek church. A reception will follow."

Chrissy heard the roar of approval coming from the hardware store at the same time as Reno squeezed her closer to him.

* * * * *

Dear Reader,

I remember reading about a holy man who was asked for the secret of his obviously contented spiritual life. He said the answer was easy. First, you keep to the Bible and, second, you deal with yourself and others with kindness.

I thought a lot about kindness while I was writing about a young woman who had made a mistake and is then surprised that people do not react to her unkindly. It has always been easier to judge a person than to bolster him or her up with kindness.

While that is particularly true for the strangers around us, it is also often easier to be harsh to ourselves than it is to be kind.

My hope is that *A Baby for Dry Creek* will remind all of us to be kinder to ourselves and to others.

Janet Tronstad

SECOND CHANCE AT LOVE

BY

IRENE BRAND

Years ago, their young marriage was torn apart by tragedy and infidelity. Yet former college sweethearts—and now Christians—Amelia Stone and Chase Ramsey were reunited while helping out victims of a severe flood. Was God giving this special couple a second chance at love?

Don't miss

SECOND CHANCE AT LOVE
On sale March 2004

Available at your favorite retail outlet.

THE
SWEETEST
GIFT

BY

JILLIAN
HART

Pilot Sam Gardner was next-door neighbor and
a friend to Kirby McKaslin when she needed
one…and the man she fell in love with. But Sam
was the one who needed Kirby to convince him
that, despite his painful past, he could have a
wonderful future—with her as his wife!

Don't miss

THE SWEETEST GIFT
On sale March 2004

Available at your favorite retail outlet.

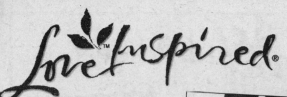

A FAMILY FOR TORY

BY

MARGARET DALEY

Victoria Alexander would do anything to help the little girl whose special needs outweighed her own—including marry the child's father! But the pain she'd seen in Slade Donovan's eyes told Tory that his daughter wasn't the only one who needed her. Could God's grace heal all their broken hearts and give Tory the family she'd always longed for?

Don't miss

A FAMILY FOR TORY

On sale March 2004

Available at your favorite retail outlet.

TWO HEARTS

BY

CYNTHIA RUTLEDGE

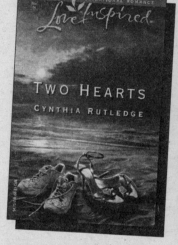

Trading places with her best friend meant wealthy
Libby Carlyle became a waitress…for extremely
handsome but stern boss Carson Davies.
When Carson noticed the beauty behind the counter,
he realized he wanted to get to know her better
and share her faith in God. But could he
trust his growing feelings and the voice inside
that urged him to believe?

Don't miss

TWO HEARTS

On sale March 2004

Available at your favorite retail outlet.